"Tortoise Reform is filled with characters that are intelligent and adorable. There is a deeper message behind this book, one of tolerance, kindness and caring."

—Debra Gaynor for Reader Views

Titles by Piers Anthony
Published by Mundania Press

ChroMagic Series
Key to Havoc
Key to Chroma
Key to Destiny
Key to Liberty
Key to Survival

Dragon's Gold Series
with Robert E. Margroff
Dragon's Gold
Serpent's Silver
Chimaera's Copper
Orc's Opal
Mouvar's Magic

Of Man and Manta Series
Omnivore
Orn
OX

Pornucopia Series
Pornucopia
The Magic Fart

Other Titles by Piers Anthony
Tortoise Reform
Macroscope

Piers Anthony Interview on Video
Conversation With An Ogre

Tortoise Reform

Piers Anthony

Mundania Press

A Mundania Press Production
Mundania Press LLC
6470A Glenway Avenue, #109
Cincinnati, Ohio 45211-5222

To order additional copies of this book, contact:
books@mundania.com
www.mundania.com

Cover Art © 2007 by SkyeWolf
SkyeWolf Images (http://www.skyewolfimages.com)
Book Design, Production, and Layout by Daniel J. Reitz, Sr.
Marketing and Promotion by Bob Sanders
Edited by Daniel J. Reitz, Sr.

Trade Paperback ISBN: 978-1-59426-379-8
eBook ISBN: 978-1-59426-378-1

First Edition • September 2007

Library of Congress Catalog Number: 2006934040

Production by Mundania Press LLC
Printed in the United States of America

10   9   8   7   6   5   4   3   2   1

Chapter 1
Strange Realm

Gopher knew he should not be digging this deep, but he was doing it anyway. He was a young unreformed tortoise, always getting into trouble. He just couldn't help it. He simply *had* to know what was beyond the next bush, or below the next layer of earth. Curiosity was his nature.

This time he was going deeper than ever before, way past the level that no sensible tortoise went beyond. In fact he was feeling dizzy with the depth. He knew he should turn around and return to the surface, and he would—after one more delve. Maybe two more.

He couldn't help remembering the scary stories about creatures who dug too deep. Like the one about the armadillo who went straight down, and never came up again. That hole was still supposed to be there, dark and menacing, avoided by all sensible creatures. Careless mice were said to fall into it, so deep that their terrified squeaking could no longer be heard. Oddly, no one Gopher knew could say exactly where that dread hole was. Just to stay well away from it.

So he was nervous as he dug. But his hole was slanting, not going straight down, and it spiraled, so he would not drift into another tortoise's burrow by accident. So it should be all right. He hoped.

Suddenly his front claw broke through to something different, startling him. Was this The Hole? No it couldn't be, because that went straight down, and this was just a spot below his tunnel. There was a pocket or a gap here; he caught a whiff of fresh air. How could that be? He was way deeper than any breeze could be. This was really curious.

He should probably leave it alone, lest it be dangerous. There were also stories about monsters of the deep, who gobbled up anyone who fell into their dens. They were supposed to have huge teeth that could crunch right through a tortoise's shell. But Gopher didn't believe that. Much.

Maybe he should check very carefully, ready to retreat the moment that danger appeared. He could scramble pretty fast when he had to.

He dug it out, opening a space so he could peer down. There was very little light here, but his nose told him that there was definitely moving air, with traces of pollen and dust. Surface air. No smell of monster, not that he knew what such a monster would smell like.

He angled his head to listen. A chunk of dirt dropped into the hole and splattered below. From that he could tell that this was a cave. He had thought he was too deep for caves, but maybe not.

He widened the hole farther so he could poke his head down into it. His shell was securely wedged against the sides, so that he could not fall. He stretched his neck down.

Suddenly ground gave way beneath him, and he dropped into the cave. He jerked in his head and legs, protecting them from harm. He had misjudged the firmness of the earth, and it had given way. Stupid mistake!

He landed with a jarring thunk. Fortunately it had not been a long fall, and he wasn't hurt, just shaken. He remained in his shell for a while, just to be sure, then cautiously poked his snout out.

He was in the cave. It extended to either side, and the air he had smelled coursed gently along it. In the ceiling was a hole: the end of his burrow. That was where he needed to go to return home. And he couldn't reach it.

He tried pawing at the side, but that turned out to be solid stone. He tried to scramble up, but it was too steep.

He walked along the cave floor a little way, to see if there was some other way to get back up to his burrow, but couldn't find any.

Gopher was in trouble. If a monster lived here...

He thought about it a moment. He had two options: to panic or to find another way home. The first was very tempting at the moment, but perhaps not a good idea. So he would try the second, hoping that his smell was correct about there being no monster. Still, he couldn't help wondering *why* that deep-delving armadillo had not returned.

He turned and trotted upwind, because that was where the cave would reach the surface. The floor of the cave angled slightly upward, confirming that this was the proper direction. It might be a long way around, because he was very deep, but in time he could do it. He hoped his burrow mates would not miss him and come searching, because one of them might fall through the hole as he had. One lost person was more than enough!

The cave turned out not to be deep after all, and soon he saw the light of the surface. That was odd, because he knew he had delved much farther down. But it would make his return easier. He could simply walk along the ground until he reached his burrow entrance.

Why did he fear that it would not be that easy?

When he reached the mouth of the cave he discovered why the surface had seem so close: it opened into a deep sink hole, where a larger cave had collapsed and laid its secrets open to the sky. This was merely an offshoot. He had some climbing to do. But he wondered, because he knew all the features of the land around his burrow, and there was no hole in the ground like this anywhere near. He had of course been digging his passage at an angle; he must have gone farther out than he intended. It was hard to maintain a perfect spiral; it was bound to drift somewhat. Still, this was weird.

He took a bite of the wire grass growing at the bottom of the sink hole. It was edible, though he could tell by the texture that it was not growing rapidly, because there was not enough water. That suggested drought, and was another indication of the distance this place was from home, because there had been good recent rain near his burrow. In fact, there had been danger of flooding.

He started in, scrambling up the steep slope. His moving feet made little avalanches behind. He got hot and had to rest a while; then he continued until he reached the top.

Now he could see the landscape—and he paused with amazement. It was completely unfamiliar. There were trees and gullies and glades thick with bushes, just as there were at home, but these were *different* trees, gullies, glades and bushes. He had never been here before.

He must have traveled much farther than he had realized. How was he going to find his way home, when he had no idea where he was?

There seemed to be no help for it but to start looking. If he went far enough, he was bound to intersect familiar territory, and then he would know his way home. But how much easier it would be if he only had Owl along!

He started questing, spiraling out from the great sink hole, because he did not know what direction was most likely. This promised to be a long, wearing search. Cottontail could have done it much faster—but Cottontail wasn't here either.

Along the way he took bites of the local foliage. All of it was dry, but he could handle that. There was bound to be something more succulent somewhere. All he had to do was find a spring or river.

About halfway around the sink hole he spied something in the distance that made him pause. It was not a tree or a pile of rocks, but seemed to be something in between. It was roughly square, or cubical, with odd facets. He had never seen anything quite like it before. So he paused to contemplate it for a while. He needed a rest anyway, having gotten hot from exertion again.

After a time something came from the structure. It was an animal of some type, taller than long. In fact it was a small human. So that must be a human den. But this human was as odd as its den, for it was covered with leaves or fur. No, it was cloth, but not one of the standard cloaks that service humans wore. This had no pattern; it was a confused mixture.

This must be a wild human. That meant that this place was truly far away, for there were no wild humans in the local forest. Any wild ones who strayed near were quickly captured and tamed, for there was always menial work to be done.

Gopher had a sudden idea. Why not capture and tame this human, and make it lift him up to his burrow hole in the cave? Then he could return the way he came.

He headed for the human, who was moving toward a copse of trees. He adjusted his angle to intersect the human at that copse, and also to conceal himself, for wild humans did not necessarily like to be tamed. He had to get close enough to it to dominate its mind before it realized he was there. Otherwise it might flee, and he might never be able to catch it. Wild creatures were notoriously skittish.

As he circled around some brush, he spied a raccoon. Raccoons were smart animals, smarter than just about any other. Maybe he could get advice from it about where he was lost. So he swerved to intersect it, coming within the mind range of sapient strangers. The creature ignored him, which was impolite but not unusual; raccoons tended to hold slower creatures in unwarranted contempt. "Hail!" he thought strongly.

The raccoon paused. It turned its head to peer at him. It was a male of medium age. It's mind seemed to be blank.

"Hail, Raccoon," Gopher repeated. "I wish to consult."

The creature drew back, its mind startled. Then it turned and ran away.

Gopher stared after it, astonished. This was a severe breach of social form. The creature had reacted like an unintelligent brute, fearing the mind contact. Indeed, Gopher had detected no intelligence. It must have been a defective animal, one that had never become civilized.

Or else this realm was even stranger than he had thought.

He moved on toward the copse. The human was no

longer in view, but he extended his awareness and picked up a faint trace in the vicinity of the copse. That was surely it.

In time he reached the copse. The human mental trace was stronger; the creature was not moving. That was convenient, because that species could move much faster than a tortoise. In fact the human was lying down, its face buried in a patch of moss. It was easy to come within full mind range.

But as he did so, he was surprised. This creature was suffering strong emotion. It seemed to be loneliness and sorrow. That was unusual, for humans were normally not much given to feelings other than pain, hunger, or satisfaction. They lacked the wit to support complex emotions. In addition, this was a young one, female, and not aggressive. And—could it be believed? *She had a complex mind!*

Gopher paused for some time, assimilating that. He must be mistaken, for no human had such a mind. They were all beasts of burden, unable ever to rise to complex thought. Useful in their place, but always as beasts.

He needed to verify this. He extended his mind. "Human," he thought forcefully. "Human: respond to me."

The creature lifted her head and oriented on him. Her face was wet. Her eyes had been watering copiously, soaking the moss beneath and spreading moisture around. From her sorrow; it was a peculiarity of the species.

"A turtle!" she thought, suddenly pleased. "Hello, turtle." The odd thing was that she accompanied her thoughts with vocal noises.

Turtle? How could such a gross confusion arise? But at the moment he had to focus on the mental contact.

"Hello, human," Gopher replied. "Are you sapient?" This was impossible, but he had to test it.

"Sapient? You mean smart. Sure I'm smart enough. Is that really you talking to me, or am I dreaming?"

This was yet another surprise. "You can dream?"

"Sure. Who doesn't?" She sat up and focused more intently on him. "I can't really be talking to a turtle! They don't have smart minds."

"Of course they do," Gopher thought. "It is humans who lack complex minds."

She laughed, another startling thing. "What could you come from, where turtles are smart and humans are dull?"

"I am not a turtle!" Gopher snapped. "I am a gopher tortoise. Don't you know the difference?"

She gazed at him, surprised. "Yes, I guess I do know the difference. I just wasn't thinking. Turtles swim, tortoises walk on land. I'm sorry." She looked away, then back to him as if expecting him to disappear. "I just can't believe you're talking to me."

"That is the nature of my realm," Gopher replied, taken aback that *she* should think *he* could be stupid. Everything about this realm was surprising. But it did seem that this human was indeed smart.

And the raccoon had been dull. Could this be the nature of this realm? A reversal of the natural order?

"So you're a tortoise," she said. "But then why are you called a gopher? That's a rodent, I think, not a reptile."

"We are called gophers because we dig burrows. We are not rodents. We are the only tortoises who do burrow. We are the landlords of our burrows, making places for other sapient animals, so we have a certain authority."

"You mean like the head of the household?"

Her mental concept seemed reasonably accurate. "Yes."

She clapped her two hands together. "So you're someone important. That's great."

She kept surprising him. He had never thought of himself as important, but it was a pleasant concept. "Human, are all members of your species like you?" he asked.

She shook her head, yet another unusual gesture. "Of course not. We're all different. Except that we're all smarter than any of the animals are."

"In my realm all humans are dull," Gopher explained. "I have never before encountered a smart human."

"And I never met a smart tortoise," she thought. "This is weird. Where exactly *is* your realm?"

"I am not sure. I was delving deep, and I fell into a

cave. When I emerged on the surface, I was here, in this remarkably odd region."

"You didn't fall out of an alien spaceship or something?"

Gopher paused, trying to make sense of the concept. It seemed to involve some kind of flying rock in which small green creatures lurked. "I did not do this thing," he agreed after a moment.

"Gee, this is interesting," she said. "Will you show me where you were in the cave?"

"It was my intention to have you go there and lift me to my burrow exit. But I assumed you were a beast of burden. Your sapience complicates the situation."

"I'll bet!" She got to her feet. "Is it far away?"

"It will take me some time to return there."

"I don't think I have that kind of time. I have to be back for supper soon. Is it okay if I carry you?"

"This is the normal function of a beast of burden. But I am not certain it is appropriate for a smart individual. Especially an untamed one."

"Oh come on, Tortoise! This is my realm. We tame animals the way I guess you tame humans. I can do what I want, if it's okay with you."

"In that case, agreed. Carry me, carefully."

"I will," she agreed. She bent down to put her two hands on his shell, and lifted him into the air.

"Alarm!" Gopher thought as he swayed dizzily.

She paused. "What's the matter?"

"This is not secure conveyance."

"Oh, you mean I'm carrying you wrong? I have a good hold on your shell. How else can I do it?"

"We normally use a howdah."

"A what?"

Gopher projected a picture of the standard howdah: a railed platform just above the head of a human beast, supported by wooden rods attached to a harness about the creature's shoulders. This enabled a tortoise or other sapient animal to ride securely, with the best view of the surroundings. Because it was near the head of the beast, it was able to direct even the dullest one quite readily.

"Neat!" she said. Gopher was picking up her nuances of expression; it was her thoughts he read, but she thought of this as speaking, and made accompanying sounds. "You really ride in style. But I don't have a howdah."

She had a point "Then carry me as steadily as possible."

"Now where's your cave?"

"You are walking toward it. I am directing you."

"You are? I thought I was just going anywhere."

"Geographic directions need not be conscious. We normally do not inform our carriers where we are going. They have no interest in that sort of thing."

"This is weird! It's the way we guide horses."

"What is this beast?"

She sent a mental picture of a truly huge animal, bigger than a deer, with a human straddling its back. "So you see," she said, "We do it too, only we call them saddles, not howdahs." Then she remembered something; Gopher felt the new thought surge into her mind. "Elephants! *They* have howdahs!" She made another picture, this time of an animal much larger than the horse, with a pendulous dangling nose.

This was too much for Gopher to assimilate, so he changed the subject. "Do you have a personal designation, to distinguish you from others of your kind?"

"Sure. I'm Rowan, after the rowan tree, with red berries. At least it's supposed to have; I've never seen one. And what's your name?"

"I am Gopher, of my local burrow. Gopher Tortoise."

"The same way I'm Rowan Human," she said, laughing.

Gopher did not properly understand this reaction, so he changed the subject again. "What other species govern your realm?"

She was blank. "Other species?"

"In our realm, a number of species are sapient. What other sapient creatures share your realm?"

"No other species. We're the only one. Maybe there are aliens from space or something who are as smart as us, but we haven't met any of those yet, so it's just us."

"Only one? Then what do you do for burrow mates?"

"Burrow mates?"

"The other sapient creatures who share your burrow."

"Oh, you mean like family and friends. We just have other people in our houses, and maybe some pets. Who do you share with?"

"Four other sapient animals share my burrow: a rabbit, a snake, an armadillo, and an owl. We are looking for one more to complete our complement. Then we can apply for status as a formal burrow, and reserve the land around us for our purposes."

"Purposes?"

"We need to forage for food, and to keep foreign predators at bay. Our lives will be more comfortable."

"Oh, I see. The same way we own land, so the other humans have to stay off, and we can grow our gardens or whatever."

They continued to compare notes as they moved, and to understand each other's realms better. But there was one thing Gopher still did not comprehend. "Why were you so unhappy, when I encountered you?"

"Oh, that! It doesn't matter now."

"I do not understand."

"I was crying because I was so lonely. Here I am, stuck with relatives I hardly know while my folks sort out their problems far away. I'm in a strange house, with no friends. I just went out somewhere to lie down and cry. But then you came, and now maybe I have a friend, and least until you go back to your home. So I'm okay now, but I'll be lonely again soon."

"What is a friend?"

"Someone you know who cares about you."

"You have no close associates of your own kind?"

"Not here. Not yet. I guess they'll come, in time, but meanwhile it's rough." She glanced down at him, still held by her two prehensile hands. "And of course I know you're not really a friend, you're a tortoise. But you feel like a friend, so that's fine."

"Perhaps it is similar to the way I feel about my burrow mates," Gopher thought. "I value them, and am bound to help them in way way I can, and they feel the same about me. We are all unified against others."

"Your burrow mates really are different animals? Rabbits and things? What about other tortoises?"

"I stand with my burrow mates. There will be no other tortoises in my burrow."

"And you said there's an owl, and a snake? I thought owls eat snakes."

"Not a burrow mate!" Gopher replied, shocked. "We protect one another."

"Sounds like friendship to me. How would you feel if you lost a burrow mate?"

"That would be a tragedy. We would have to get another, and that would be awkward. Individuals are not interchangeable."

"That is so right!"

While they talked, the girl had been moving toward the cave, climbing down the slope of the sink hole. She was much better at it than Gopher had been, because she could take big steps and keep her balance. That was of course why humans made excellent beasts of burden; they had the bodies for it. Now they were at the bottom—and there was the cave.

"Wow! I never knew there was a cave here. Of course I haven't had time to explore." She walked into it, ducking her head to get past the low spots. "But it's pretty dark in here. Maybe I should go to the house and fetch a light."

Gopher had no idea how she could do such a thing, and at this point just wanted to get back to his burrow. "I will guide you, and warn you of any stumble points. When you return you will be going toward the light, so should not have trouble."

"Okay." She carried him on, and soon enough they were there. Gopher spied the hole where his burrow tunnel had broken through to the cave. Following his guidance, she stopped directly beneath it and lifted him up. In a moment his feet caught at the edges, and he was able to scramble up into it.

"Appreciation," he thought back at her. "You have saved me much mischief."

"Will I see you again, Gopher?" she asked. "I'd really like to. I like you better than anyone I've met here."

"I can return tomorrow if you like. This is an interesting realm."

"Not half as interesting as yours! I'd like to meet your owl friend, too. I like birds."

"I will bring Owl along. Tomorrow at midday."

"Great!" she exclaimed. "I'll be here right then. And I won't tell a soul, 'cause nobody would believe me anyway, and I'd rather have a great secret."

Gopher moved on up the burrow tunnel, leaving her behind. Gradually her mental trace diminished, fading with distance.

Now the significance of what he had found weighed more heavily. A whole new realm! Where animals were stupid, and humans were smart. That would surely amaze his burrow mates.

But there was something else. The human, Rowan Girl, was not just an example of a weird situation; she was a nice person. She had helped him return, and introduced him to the concept of friendship. She was like a burrow mate, only not one. He had had close mental contact with her, and gotten to know she was genuine. He liked her, and he had never before liked any non-burrow mate, let alone any beast of burden. So he must indeed be her friend.

He had agreed to return the next day, and he would, because this new realm was fascinating. But also because he wanted to meet Rowan again, and show her to Owl. Gopher moved on up the burrow tunnel, leaving her behind. Her mental trace was very faint, and then it was gone.

Chapter 2
Trouble

It was the largest, fattest, juiciest mouse he had ever seen. He pounced on it, caught it, and swallowed it whole. And there before him was another mouse, even fatter and slower. He focused on it—

"Burrow Meeting."

Owl woke with a start. Why did these things always have to happen when he was in the middle of the best dreams? He shook himself, then hauled himself out of his cubby and down the tunnel to the main chamber. Day was almost over anyway, and soon enough he would be out in the dusk hunting real mice.

The others were already there. Now Owl picked up the aura of excitement. Gopher had something important to tell them. Had he found a good prospect for a sixth burrow mate?

It turned out to be something astonishingly different. "I have found a new realm!" the tortoise thought. "One that looks like ours, but where the animals are stupid and the humans are smart."

There was a rush of surprise. None of the animals had ever thought of such a thing. Humans were beasts of burden, quite useful for that, but none of them were sapient.

"Have you been dreaming?" Indigo's thought inquired.

"No, just burrowing deep," Gopher replied.

"Maybe one of us should check that tunnel," Owl thought. "Dreams can seem quite real on occasion, especially if you are tired."

"Exactly," Gopher agreed. "I hardly believe it myself. I met a native there, and promised to return tomorrow, and to bring you along."

Owl realized that he should have kept his mind shut. Now he was committed. "I will go," he agreed.

"You met a native?" Cottontail inquired. "Of what nature?"

"Human. Female. Young. Smart."

There was general surprise. "The first three I understand," Indigo thought. "But smart? You mean smart for her type?"

"I mean smart like an animal," Gopher clarified. "As smart as any of us, perhaps smarter."

They were amazed. "I think we all would like to see this smart beast," Peba thought. "Are you quite sure you weren't dreaming?"

"Not absolutely sure," Gopher replied. "That is why I want verification by a burrow mate. But I believe it is true."

Owl and the others saw this in his mind, and had to believe. Of course burrow mates always accepted the news and beliefs of their fellows. But this was so astonishing that it did have to be verified. Gopher might have been deceived in some way. Tortoises were great burrowers, but not the smartest creatures when it came to things beyond the burrow.

Now the evening was advancing, and they had things to do. Owl made his way out of the burrow, looked around, and took wing. Late day and early evening was his best hunting time, that being when the day creatures were settling down and the night creatures were coming out.

Owl did not catch as fat a mouse as he had dreamed of, but it was sufficient. He returned early to the burrow, to get rested for the early start tomorrow.

As he settled down in his comfortable chamber, lined with feathers, grass, and the remains of prey, he pondered Gopher's strange revelation. A smart human? That seemed impossible, yet it must be so. Meeting her should be a truly novel experience. In fact, seeing that weird realm would be amazing. He looked forward to it.

Burrowing Owl relaxed and slept. Of course he dreamed, of a huge sapient human refusing to be a proper beast of burden. What would their society come to, if anything like that ever really happened? It was unnerving.

~≈

Next day, shortly before noon, Gopher led Owl down the long tunnel he had dug the day before. Actually he had been working on it for several days, just to see how far down he could go. Of course there was no point in delving so deep, which was why sensible tortoises and armadillos didn't do it. But Gopher was not sensible. None of them in this burrow were. They were all wild youths, looking for adventure before having to settle down to plodding adult life. They were all unreformed. That was one reason why they were having trouble enlisting their sixth burrow mate: smart animals were wary of such a rambunctious crew.

They went deeper than owl had ever been before, and that made him nervous. The security of a regular burrow was one thing, but this seemed like a tunnel to nowhere. And if there really was a strange other realm at its end—

Gopher slowed, then halted. "We are here," he thought. Then he send out a stronger thought. "Rowan Girl! Are you present?"

Owl almost hoped there would be no answer. But in a moment it came, a thought from a stranger. "Yes, Gopher! I was afraid you wouldn't come, and that I'd have to stop believing in you."

It was definitely the human and her thought seemed smart. Owl felt troubled. This was worse than the scary deep tunnel. A sapient human was more than unusual; it might be dangerous.

"I brought Owl," Gopher thought. "Will you help us down?"

"Sure." Now owl heard the vibration of air; the creature was making vocal sounds as she thought! Who had ever imagined such a thing? Tame humans were taught not to make such sounds, lest they interfere with the animals' awareness of the forest.

Gopher dropped slowly down into the cave below. Owl peered down and saw that the human was lifting him down to the floor. At least she was normal in that respect, doing the bidding of a sapient animal. But the rest was weird. For one thing, she was drastically out of uniform, covered in brightly colored cloth. For another, she was friendly. Human beasts of burden were normally sullen or neutral.

The girl set Gopher down, then reached up to the hole again. "I will descend myself!" Owl thought quickly, and dropped down, spreading his wings so as to land safely beside Gopher. He did not want this untamed human's hands on him. Gopher might trust her, but Owl was wary.

"Oh, you're cute!" the human thought. "I never saw such a little owl!"

Owl was taken aback. "I am a full-size burrowing owl," he responded curtly. "I am *not* cute."

She was immediately contrite. "I'm sorry. I thought—I've seen bigger owls—"

"Other species are larger, of course. But they do not burrow."

"I guess that's it. I'm not expert on owls. I meant no harm. I apologize."

"Accepted," Owl thought curtly. What else could he do? But he remained wary of this creature.

"Rowan Girl does not know our ways," Gopher thought. "She means well."

"Of course," Owl agreed gruffly.

"Do you want me to carry you out?" Rowan asked.

"Yes," Gopher replied.

"No," Owl thought.

The girl picked Gopher up and walked through the cave. Owl ran along behind. He could move faster than the tortoise on the ground, and much faster in the air.

"I'm so glad you came back," the girl said. "I was lonely without you."

"But we met only yesterday," Gopher protested.

"I was lonely before you came. But then I had someone to talk with. And now there's Owl, and he talks too. That makes two friends."

"Friend?" Owl inquired skeptically.

"Her concept is similar to burrow mates," Gopher explained. "She doesn't live in a burrow, but she does want companionship."

"Humans have never been companions for animals," Owl pointed out. "They are beasts of burden, useful in their place but hardly intellectual associates." Yet he knew as he thought that thought that the mere existence of this human girl threw all that into question. He remained disquieted.

"This is a different realm," Gopher reminded him. "Here they lack burrows but do have friends. She is sapient, so is not the same as an ordinary human."

Owl did not deign to argue the case.

The cave opened out into a huge sink hole. "Where did this come from?" Owl asked, astonished.

"This is a different realm," Gopher repeated. "Its geography is different from ours."

So it certainly seemed. "I will explore," Owl said. He spread his wings and took off into the sky.

In moments he rose above the rim of the sink hole, and the larger vista opened out beneath him. Gopher was right: this was a different realm, one Owl had never seen before. Its vegetation was similar, and the general lay of the land, but its details were foreign. For one thing there were odd boxes scattered about, and strange level stretches. What were these?

"They are houses and roads," Gopher replied to his thought. "I learned this from Rowan."

Of course the native would know. "Perhaps I should connect to her mind directly," Owl thought. It rankled him to make the suggestion, but he wanted to understand what he was seeing, and it made sense to learn from the one who knew.

"She is not used to distance mind contact," Gopher thought. "She needs experience. We must teach her how to project."

"Hmpf," Owl thought. But what could one expect of a

human? The fact that she thought at all was remarkable enough.

He flew in a widening spiral, surveying the land. Satisfied that it was unfamiliar as far as he could see, he turned back and glided down into the sink hole.

Meanwhile the girl had carried Gopher up to the rim of the sink hole, and he was grazing on some of the grass that rimmed it. Tortoises had to eat a lot, their food being far less concentrated and nutritious than live mice.

Rowan glanced at her wrist. "Oops—I have to go to the house for lunch," she said. "My aunt will be suspicious if I'm late. I'll come back in an hour, I promise."

"We shall wait for you," Gopher agreed.

"Great!" She took off running toward the nearest of the cubic structures Owl had noted.

"What is this 'hour' she mentioned?" Owl thought.

"A measure of time, a fraction of a day. She will return when it is used up."

"We have to dawdle here, waiting for a human?" Owl asked, annoyed.

"Oh, come on, Owl—you know you like her."

"She's human!"

"She's *sapient* human. That makes all the difference."

He was right, but Owl didn't want to admit it right away. "I will use the time to explore further."

"And I will use it to fill my belly," Gopher agreed. Tortoises were also more placid than owls; it came with their plodding nature.

"And owls are flighty," Gopher agreed with good humor.

Owl took off again. This time he flew over the human girl's head. She glanced up, seeing him, and lifted her arm in a clumsy wave. She was so foolishly friendly! Then Owl was on ahead, passing over the "house." It was a big structure, with weirdly reflective panels on the sides. Humans had made this thing? But of course humans didn't like to live in burrows for some reason, so they did fashion crude structures in the forest. It was part of their dull lifestyle.

There was a "road" passing near the house—and

something was moving on it. Owl peered at the thing, surprised. It was a box, like the house, only smaller, sliding rapidly along the road. When the road curved, the box stayed with it, like a mouse running along a path. But this box was much larger than a mouse; it was only the perspective of distance that made it seem small.

Owl followed the moving box, and soon it approached another box going the opposite direction. They raced right toward each other, like two goats about to butt heads, but they passed each other by the barest of margins. What a curious process!

Owl watched the moving boxes for some time, and saw that they weren't really trying to butt heads; each stayed on one side of the road, and there was just room for them to pass. But the whole thing remained curious, because they weren't alive. They were metallic objects zooming along. He had realized that this realm was unfamiliar, before, but thought it was just geography; now he knew that it was far odder than that. Maybe the human girl would know what these things were, and what business they were going about. Did they have to travel to metallic pastures to graze?

He swooped low to study the situation more closely. He passed a tree, and saw several birds on the ground near it. They were of sapient size, chickens, so he paused to hail them.

But the moment they saw him, the chickens fled, squawking. "I'm not hunting you," he thought to them. "I merely wish to exchange news." Because as a rule sapients did not hunt sapients. It was bad form, for one thing, and it could be dangerous. Chickens were not the smartest of birds, but they did know the conventions.

But the chickens would not exchange thoughts. No, it was worse; he discovered that they *had* no sapient thoughts. Their minds were dull. So it was true: animals in this realm were stupid. Gopher had said they were, but Owl had not experienced it for himself. What a tragedy!

He ascended, leaving the dull chickens below. He saw other birds, but they were small ones, below the threshold of sapience anyway. Suddenly he was feeling lonely. How awful it would be to live in a realm where all the other animals were dull!

Then Owl spied something in the distant air, flying extremely high. It was a big bird, a huge bird—no, it was too big to be any bird. It was another metallic thing, this time traveling in the sky. That was daunting, because Owl had thought himself safe from pursuit by the boxes. But if some of them could fly, nowhere was safe.

He felt a faint signal of alarm. For a moment he thought it was his own. Then he recognized the trace: it was Gopher. Gopher was in trouble. They were separated too far for him to read any more than that, but he knew he had to get back immediately. He looped around.

But that big flying box was there. He did not want to approach it, lest it try to crash into him. He tried to fly around it, but the thing was coming toward him at what turned out to be impossible speed. Now it was making a noise, like that of ten bears growling together, only less personal.

Owl dived for the nearest tree below. He caught a branch and tried to hide amidst the foliage as the flying box loomed loudly close. Then it was going away. He had escaped it.

He lurched back into the air and looked after the box. It was already far away, and now he saw that it was still well high in the sky, descending slowly. There had really been no danger of collision.

Feeling shaken and somewhat foolish, he flew back toward the sink hole and Gopher. The tortoise was still emanating alarm, and was hiding inside his shell. But he did not seem to be physically hurting. What had happened?

It took a while to get back, for owl had flown farther than he realized while watching the boxes on the road. When he came to land at the rim of the sink hole, Gopher wasn't there. His traces were there—his smell and his tracks—but not his body. His mind was some distance away, farther than he could have walked in the time he had been alone. Where had he gone, and how?

Alarmed anew, Owl took to the air and flew around

the sink hole, searching. But Gopher simply was not there, as his mental trace indicated.

Then Owl saw the human girl running from the house. He was relieved to see her. She was not his preference for company, but she might have some notion what had happened and what to do about it. He flew toward her.

"Hi, Owl!" she called as she saw him. She lifted her hand. "Come land on me, if you want to."

Owl, confused, did something he had had no intention of doing: he dropped down and landed on her shoulder. He took hold, not hard, for his claws were strong and sharp, and human flesh was notoriously fragile. "Gopher is gone!" he thought.

"I heard you!" she said, thrilled. He felt her good feeling, and that made him feel good too, somewhat against his will. Mind contact conveyed more than just direct thoughts; it framed them with background information and emotion. Because he was in actual physical contact with her, communication was good despite her poorly developed mind ability. At a reasonable distance he would receive only her specific thoughts, and beyond that very little, because he hardly knew her. The better the acquaintance, the farther the mind contact, as a general rule.

But this was not a time for good feeling. "Gopher is gone," he repeated. "He is frightened."

Now her emotion changed to dismay. "Oh, I was so glad to hear you I didn't pick up on what you said. I only really talked to Gopher before. You were sort of, well, aloof. Why did Gopher go? I said I would come back, and I did."

"It was not voluntary," Owl clarified. "Something happened to him."

"Oh, no! What did it?"

"I was not present. I felt his alarm, but was too far away to get his full thought. I returned, but he was gone."

They reached the rim of the sink hole. "You're right. He's not here. He was grazing right in this patch, and—uh-oh." Her thought turned dark.

"What is it?"

"There's footprints here. See, right in the dirt. Some man must have picked him up and taken him away."

"A human male? Maybe Gopher directed him to do it." But Owl did not believe that.

"I think I know," Rowan said. "Uncle was talking about it just at lunch. He says there's some huge development going to be made here. They're going to fill in the sink hole and bulldoze out the trees and build it. He says by this time next year we won't even recognize the place. But the first thing they have to do is move out the tortoises, 'cause they're a protected species, something like that. So they must be collecting them and taking them to some other place, and that's what's happened to Gopher."

"But Gopher is not of this realm," Owl protested. He hardly understood the business about something huge being made, but Gopher's absence was all too clear.

"They don't know that. They must think he's a regular tortoise. They don't know he's telepathic. They must have him in a pen somewhere, ready to ship off to the new location."

Obviously she knew far more about this matter than Owl did. "What can we do?"

"We can rescue him, that's what," she said. "If we can find him."

"I have his mental trace. I can find him. But I can not remove him from a pen." For her mental picture was of a metallic enclosure without an exit.

"We'll do it together," she said. "You find him, I'll rescue him." She paused. "But maybe not by day. If they see me, they'll stop me. I'll have to sneak out at night and do it. Can you find him in the dark?"

"I am an owl," Owl reminded her stiffly.

"Oh, sure, yes, of course. I forgot. So can you wait until evening?"

"Perhaps I should return to the burrow and inform the others. Then I can come back here."

"Okay. Let's meet right here. I'll bring a flashlight." Then she sent a pang of nervousness. "But please *do* come back, because I'll have no idea where to go otherwise."

"I would not desert a burrow mate. That is never done."

She tilted her head in a nod. Gopher was right: she

had peculiar yet somehow engaging mannerisms, for a human. "It sounds nice, in your burrow."

"Nice is hardly the applicable term. We are an essential group. We derive our strength from that unity, becoming much more than we would ever be alone."

"Different creatures? That seems odd—but still nice."

"That is the custom. A normal burrow has six sapients selected from creatures of appropriate size. The tortoise is the landlord, because he makes the burrow. The others contribute their special skills to it, making the whole."

"Who is there, besides you and Gopher? I mean, their names."

"Indigo Snake, Peba Armadillo, and Cottontail Rabbit. Now I must fly there and inform them."

"Of course," she agreed wistfully. "I wish I could see your burrow sometime."

That was obviously impossible, so Owl did not respond. He spread his wings and departed her shoulder.

"Bye!" she thought after him. Then he was beyond her range and on his own.

He dived into the sink hole and zoomed into the cave. He found the hole and scrambled into the tunnel Gopher had made. Soon he would be there in the burrow proper.

What a story he had to tell them!

Chapter 3
Rescue

Rowan's feelings were severely mixed as she walked slowly back toward the house. She was exhilarated to have met such interesting and personal creatures: a telepathic tortoise and owl. But she was horrified that Gopher had been kidnapped, or tortoise-napped. All because of that stupid development they were planning.

Then she thought of something else. They were going to fill in the sink hole! That meant that the cave that led to the other world would be covered over, and the smart animals would no longer be able to visit her. Then her life would sink right back into the dull lonely awfulness it had been two days ago. She wouldn't be able to bear it. It was bad enough with the problem back home, so that she had been cast out into this emotional wilderness. Now she was going to be denied her only real friends here.

For they were indeed friends. She knew that because she had exchanged minds with them, a little. She wasn't good at it, but she was learning. She couldn't do distance yet, but when one of them was close to her head she knew that creature better than she could know any human person. That was the way it was, with telepathy, because it included pictures and feelings as well as words. A person couldn't lie; the truth was always there. So she had trusted Gopher and he had trusted her, from the outset. Gopher was real nice, and Owl was crusty but okay after a bit. He just had this thing about not liking strangers. He had been turned off because she thought he was cute. She still thought so, but would try to bury that so as not to aggravate him. Regardless, the sheer novelty and wonder of sharing minds was so great, she just had to have more of it. She knew she'd like the other animals in their burrow, if only she could meet them. Because of their minds. Telepathy was like coming home.

But she had a big problem to work out. In a moment she knew that she faced two challenges, not one. First she had to rescue Gopher Tortoise from the abductors. Second, she had to stop that development. She had no idea how, but she knew it had to be done. Her happiness depended on it.

First things first. She should organize for the night's mission. She would lay out dark clothing and make sure her flashlight had a fresh battery. Then she would get some rest, because she was going to lose sleep in the night.

That was another problem. She didn't like deceiving Aunt and Uncle. She knew they were nice enough people. It wasn't their fault that her folks were having problems and had to farm her out for a while. In fact they were being pretty decent about boarding her. But they did not understand children, having had none of their own. Sometimes they acted as if she were a little adult, and sometimes as if she were two years old. They hadn't found the range for age ten. So they expected her to do her own chores, like laundry, which was adult, and to be in bed and asleep by nine PM, which was child. And they had no understanding at all of her need to interact with her friends.

That last was the worst. She had a slender slew of fine friends in fifth grade, and some vile villainous enemies, and had had every intention of keeping in touch with them all over the summer. Summer was a great time to do things, good and bad. The bad things could be almost as much fun as the good ones. She was good at being bad, when she tried. It was maybe her last real chance to be a tomboy before she had to start orienting on (ugh!) young lady hood.

Then, suddenly, she had been uprooted and sent here to another state where she knew nobody. But she was expected to be adult about it, knowing it was her folks' only real choice. While she really felt childish about it, hating the dreadful boredom and loneliness of life without friends. She couldn't phone, because Uncle didn't like the expense. No email either, because he didn't have a computer. She was *really* isolated. She didn't even have her favorite books along, because no one knew how long this exile was going to be. It depended on things vastly beyond her control.

Overwhelmed by it all, she had fled the house and flung herself down near the sink hole to cry her heart out, or at least as much of it as could be dissolved in tears. And met an alien tortoise. She knew he was alien, because who ever heard of one of those creatures living underground? Also, because he was telepathic. She had heard of that, but never believed it. Aliens from other planets were often telepathic, but that was just in the movies. Yet it was so, and he was really smart for a tortoise, and she liked him. So she accepted Gopher as he was, because she really needed a friend and he was what offered.

She had thought he was bluffing about having animal friends like himself. But he had brought Owl, the cutest little owl she had ever imagined, and he was smart and telepathic too. Actually they sort of had to be telepathic, because neither a snout nor a beak was suitable for talking the way human folk did. Owl was sort of reserved, almost prickly, but she liked him anyway. So now she had two friends, and she wasn't going to let them down.

She reached the house and went inside. Uncle was off at his job, and Aunt was out shopping, so she was alone—and for once she was glad of it. She went to the garage and found a flashlight. Its beam was bright, so she knew the battery was okay. She considered, then took a medium screwdriver too. If Gopher was locked in a cage, she would need to get it open. In fact maybe she should take wire cutters too, just in case.

She went to her room, which was a converted storage chamber. They weren't being mean, it was just what they had, and it was okay. She dug out her darkest jeans and shirt. And what about mosquitoes? They could be bad at night. So she went back to the garage and found a little bottle of ancient old army-surplus bug repellant. It smelled awful, and that made her smile: that was what any mosquito who tried to bite her would get a mouthful of. Served it right.

Finally she set up her heaviest dark socks, to protect her feet from both sight and scratching. And an old work cap. She hid the whole outfit under the bed. It wasn't that she didn't have a right to use it, but that she didn't want anyone to catch on to her mission. If she tried to tell them about telepathic animal friends they would think she had gone crazy. Well, if she had, she wanted to stay that way, because now the loneliness was gone.

She lay on the bunk and closed her eyes, but realized right away that she couldn't sleep. She was too excited by the challenge before her, and anyway, she hardly ever slept in the daytime. So she closed her eyes and thought about Problem Number Two: the big construction project. What was she going to do about that? She couldn't just march up to the nearest bulldozer and tell them to leave the sink hole alone because it was an avenue to telepathic animals. They would dismiss her as an imaginative child, which she was. Yet it would be worse if they believed her, and went after the smart animals. She had few illusions about what who happen to a telepathic tortoise: he would be sent to a laboratory for study, and never have his freedom again. Same for a smart owl. At best they would be put on display in some public cage for tourists to gawk at. No, she would never tell that secret!

So how was she going to do it? Because she knew it was up to her. No one else knew about the smart animals or the route to their realm. But if she couldn't tell anyone the truth, how could she do anything? That was one enormous challenge.

～⁓

She woke as she heard Aunt's car return. She had fallen asleep after all! That was just as well, because it set

her up better for the night's activity. Now if she could successfully play the innocent child so that no one suspected…

ॐॐ

Rowan dutifully went to her room and was safely in
bed exactly at nine PM with the light out. Aunt normally
didn't think to check on her, but just in case, she set pillows under the sheet to make a person-sized hump in the
bed. She put on her dark outfit in the darkness, trusting
that everything was in its proper place. Then she carefully lifted the screen out of the open window, climbed
over the sill, stood outside, and set the screen back in.
Thank goodness houses in this region were all on one
floor!

Her heart was beating like mad. Part of her mind
couldn't believe she was doing this. Another part knew
she had to. She wasn't a criminal, she just had an important job to do. She stood for a minute, getting used to it,
letting her heartbeat subside. She couldn't afford to freak
herself out.

She didn't dare use her flashlight near the house,
lest someone see the light, so she walked slowly and carefully across the yard until her feet found the brushy fringe.
Actually she could see some, as there was a bit of moon-
light, so she kept on going as she was. She had to get to
the sink hole to meet Owl.

Then she thought of something. Owl was fully telepathic, and could read her thoughts, and could pick up
on a friend from a distance. So she tried to project her
thought. She could not truly send on her own, but maybe
she could make her mind a little brighter so he could
spot it. "Owl!" she called with her mouth carefully shut.

"Coming."

She had an answer! It had worked! She was thrilled
again. It was so great to have it work.

"I was close by anyway, waiting for you," Owl thought
grumpily as he landed on her shoulder.

Oh. Still, maybe in time she would learn how to do it
at a distance. It was a weird business, using her mind
like this. She had never even tried it before.

"I agree," Owl thought. "In our realm, no human can project thought. It is remarkable that you are able to do it even crudely."

"I guess I have an open mind," Rowan thought, gratified. "Maybe it's something any person could do in our world, but nobody ever thinks to try, and by the time a person grows up, it's too late. I guess Gopher caught me just in time."

"When your mind was most open to contact."

"Yes, I guess so. I really, *really* wanted someone to talk to, who would understand. And he did."

"But it is even more remarkable that your human species is sapient," Owl thought. "We had always assumed that mind projection was an aspect of sapience or near-sapience. Now it seems that intelligence and thought projection are not always together."

"To me it is remarkable that animals are smart," Rowan said, still keeping her mouth shut. "But I'm glad you are."

"Now we have business. Are you prepared?"

"As well as I can be. I figure Gopher's in a cage somewhere, and I can pry it open and get him out. But first I have to find him."

"I will find him, and guide you to him. He is in that direction." Owl made a mental indication. It was like a faint beam of light, only it didn't illuminate anything.

"Then I'll go that way. Uh, is it far?"

"It should take you a fraction of the night."

"Can you give that to me in hours?"

Owl peered into her mind. It was a peculiar questing, like a wisp of fog winding through her head. "What is an hour? You used that term before, but I do not know how long it is."

"One twelfth of a day. From dawn to dusk is about twelve hours, on average." But she felt his confusion; Owls evidently weren't good at math. So she tried another way. "Here is my feeling about how long an hour is." She thought of how long it felt to wait an hour.

"That suffices. At your rate of walking velocity, you might get there in under an hour. But there may be obstructions."

"I'd rather use the roads and open fields, especially at night." She considered. "Look, Owl—can you play hot or cold with me?"

"Fire or snow?"

She laughed. "I mean, be encouraging when I'm going in the right direction and negative when I'm not? Hot for the right way, cold for the wrong way."

Owl digested this. Rowan felt his thought: Not only was this human sapient, her mind functioned in unusual ways. "This is feasible. Perhaps I can instill in you the appropriate direction, so you will know."

"That's good too. Gopher did that, and it worked." She turned and speeded her pace. "This way, right?"

"Correct. I will go ahead and verify Gopher's situation."

"But without you I might lose the way!"

"I will remain in contact. Orient your mind on mine." He spread his wings and left her shoulder, disappearing into the night.

Rowan tried, and found that she could. He had a bird feel to him, not exactly feathery, but—

"Avian," Owl thought. "I *am* a bird."

She chuckled. "I sorta guessed that." She peered at the dim landscape ahead. She saw it more clearly now; maybe she had picked up some of Owl's night vision along with his mind contact. No, more likely her eyes had adapted better. "Am I still going the right way?" But as she focused on it, she realized that she was drifting to the side. She *did* know the direction.

However, there was a road to her left, that went in the general direction, so she cut across to walk along it. There were no cars; this was backwoods country and not very busy. She increased her pace, walking rapidly, and drew obliquely closer to the right place.

After a time, Owl returned. "You are correct. Gopher is in a cage with several other tortoises."

"How will I know them apart?" Rowan asked, alarmed.

"The others are not sapient."

"But—" She broke off. She could tell the difference,

because she could tune in on their minds. There was only one smart tortoise in all this world, and that was Gopher.

"Correct," Owl agreed.

Now she had to leave the road and follow a dirt trail. She felt the trace getting stronger. In fact she felt Gopher; she recognized his mind. It was faint but familiar. "Gopher!" she thought as loudly as she could. "I'm coming for you!"

"I know it," Gopher answered. "Owl told me."

Oh. Of course. She felt like a dull human. But still, she had succeeded in contacting him at a distance. She was improving. It was as if she were exercising special muscles in her mind that were getting stronger as she used them. Those mind muscles might feel stiff in the morning, but it was wonderful now. His trace was getting stronger as she approached him.

The cage was in a truck parked near a lighted house. So the tortoises had not yet been delivered, and were here overnight. They were lucky; there was no telling how far away the relocation site might be.

She sneaked around the truck, so that it was between her and the house. She reached the cage. It was big, holding about eight tortoises. She felt for its door—and it was a simple latch. She didn't need the screwdriver or wire cutters after all. That was a relief. She opened it, oriented on Gopher, reached inside, and picked him up with both hands. She set him on the ground, then closed the door.

"Thank you," Gopher thought. "I was concerned."

"So was I," Owl thought.

"We weren't going to let them keep you," Rowan thought, relieved that it had after all be so easy.

Then she realized that all the tortoises were similarly captive. Should she release them all? But there were problems. She would have to carry them all far enough away to be well clear of the house and truck, or the tortoise abductors would just round them up again in the morning. And they would all be lost, because this was about three miles from the sink hole, and they could have come from anywhere. They surely wouldn't like being in unfamiliar territory any more than they would like relocation; it was really the same thing. Also, if she let them all go, the authorities would know someone had done this, and that could make trouble. They probably wouldn't miss just one tortoise. So, with regret, she left the others in the cage. After all, they were being relocated for their own good. If they stayed around the sink hole, and Rowan did not succeed in stopping the construction project, they could get killed by the bulldozers.

"I'm sorry, tortoises," she whispered, wiping away a tear. "I hope you're happy in your new digs." For she realized now that all gopher tortoises lived underground; Gopher was ordinary in that respect.

Then she picked Gopher up and walked back toward the road. Just then the door of the house opened and the dark shape of a grown man emerged. Rowan's heart leaped to her throat. She hurried behind a tree, hiding. Her pulse was pounding.

The man came out to the truck. He walked around it. "Thought I heard something," he said to himself. He looked at the cage, found it closed, and returned to the house.

Rowan's knees felt like cooked spaghetti. Suppose she had been caught with a contraband tortoise?

But it was all right. She hurried on to the road, carrying Gopher. She wanted to get back to the sink hole as fast as possible.

Owl came to land on her shoulder. "You did well, Rowan Girl," he thought. She felt the shift in his mind: he had been wary of her, but now accepted her even if she was a really odd creature.

"Thank you," she replied, flattered. "But this was only the first and lesser challenge."

"There is another problem?" Gopher asked, alarmed.

"I found out why they abducted you. They didn't know you weren't a regular tortoise, and they're clearing them all out of this region. So they can make a huge project, maybe a housing development or a superstore. The law says they have to relocate the tortoises, 'cause they're a protected species. But we have to stop that development."

"Why?" Owl asked.

"'Cause they'll fill in the sink hole and maybe pave it

over. Then there won't be any way for you to get here from your world."

"That may be best," Owl thought. "This realm is dangerous. We were lucky we were able to rescue Gopher."

"But then I won't be able to see you anymore!" she protested.

"This is important to you?" Gopher asked.

"Yes!"

"But we are not your kind," Owl thought.

"Yes you are! You're my only friends here."

"Friends?"

"The concept resembles burrow mates," Gopher explained to Owl. "She lacks associates."

"But she can't be a burrow mate."

"I wish I could be," Rowan said wistfully. "You all stand up for each other, and share your minds. It seems so nice. We don't have anything like that in this world."

"That is one of the things that makes this realm distasteful," Owl agreed.

"So you see," Rowan said. "You wouldn't want to be stuck here among the dull animals. Neither do I. I want to visit your world."

"Visit our realm!"

"She did rescue me," Gopher thought. "She should get to meet the burrow mates."

"But she can't fit through the tunnel."

"Maybe I could widen it," Rowan suggested eagerly. "If that's all right with you folk. I don't want to ruin your burrow, I just want to see your world."

"This much we might try," Gopher agreed.

Owl's objection was weakening, but not gone.

Rowan tried to follow up while she could. "And maybe your burrow mates can figure out a way to stop the project here."

"We are not certain that further contact between our realms is wise," Owl reminded her.

"Please!" she said tearfully. "My life will just end if I have to go back to dullness."

They considered. She realized with surprise that they were reacting to tears the same way human folk did, being swayed. Maybe it was because they were males.

"She did rescue me," Gopher repeated.

"She is sapient," Owl thought.

"She is learning mind communication."

"And I want to learn more," Rowan said.

"We must ask the burrow mates," Gopher decided.

Rowan saw that this was as far as they would go at this time. "Okay, ask them. And if they say we should keep the way open, then we'll have to figure out how to stop the construction."

"Agreed," Gopher and Owl thought together.

She delivered them to the cave, and carried Gopher to the burrow tunnel, using the flashlight with her free hand. She shone it up into the slanting passage. How she wished she were small enough to go there with them!

"And we'll meet here again at noon tomorrow," she said.

"Agreed," Gopher thought, and Owl made a mental wash of reluctant acceptance.

When they were gone, she made her way back to the house. She crept quietly to the window, removed the screen, climbed in, replaced the screen, and found her bed in the darkness. No one had missed her.

She undressed, got into her nightie, and into bed. She was glad she had succeeded in rescuing Gopher, and hoped they would let her visit their realm. Maybe if she got there, it wouldn't matter about the construction; it would just lock her in that other world with her friends.

꿈

Next day she was there, hoping for good news. She was early, in her eagerness and concern. Suppose they decided to let the tunnel between worlds be sealed over? That was their right, but how she hoped they would go the other way.

Now she wondered: she had her watch, just a cheap thing, but it kept reasonable time. So she knew when noon was. But how did *they* know? They did not have watches, or even any concept what an hour was, until she told them. Maybe they knew when the sun was directly overhead.

While she waited, she worked on the ramp, making it easier for Gopher or any other animal his general size to reach the floor of the cave from the tunnel. She wanted to encourage them any which way she could.

At last there was a sifting of dirt, and Gopher appeared. "What's the answer?" she cried. "Will you keep the way open?"

"We have not decided," he replied gravely. "It is too big a decision for us, since we lack a really smart burrow mate."

"Smart? But all of you are smart, aren't you?"

"We are all smarter than beasts," he agreed. "But there are differences. Each has his specialty. I can burrow well, and so can Peba."

"Who?"

"Peba Armadillo. Owl can fly. Cottontail Rabbit can move rapidly and far. Indigo Snake can slither into crevices none of the rest of us can reach. But none of us specialize in being smart. We need a raccoon, or a small fox, but so far we have not found one who wants to share our burrow. So we are not yet official, and we lack the intelligence to really handle a question like this."

"I'm sorry," she said.

"So we decided to hold a burrow meeting with you, exploring it, and then decide."

"That's fair," she said, relieved that they hadn't decided no. "But how can I get to your burrow? That tunnel isn't nearly big enough for me."

"We have come here."

"Right now?" she asked, amazed.

"Yes, if you are willing."

"Oh, yes!" she cried gladly.

"Then we shall come down, and view your realm, and think with you, and decide."

"Yes! Yes!" she cried, clapping her hands in girlish glee. They were going to give it a fair chance. She was totally thrilled.

Chapter 4
Revelation

Indigo Snake was not thrilled by this wild notion of Gopher's, but Owl supported him and a creature did have to humor the notions of any burrow mate. Especially the burrow landlord. However, Indigo was curious about this mysterious portal to another realm, even if he didn't quite believe it. So he slithered along with the others to make the arranged meeting. Maybe the supposedly smart human girl would not show up, and they would be free to go about their own businesses. Then they would be in the safe position of having supported Gopher without getting their lives disrupted.

But when they reached the hole into the nether cave, there she was: a half-grown human child garbed just as oddly as Gopher had thought. Her thoughts were all over, excited, hopeful, eager; Indigo had to damp down his reception as he came close, so as not to get confused by her undisciplined enthusiasm. Children were so—so excitable.

Gopher thought with her, and Indigo appreciated that the human child really did have telepathic ability. It was crude and untrained, but had potential once she got it under control. That alone was remarkable; there had never before been a human with more than the dull ability to receive tightly focused thought-commands. So obviously this realm was different in that important respect.

They moved down the dirt ramp to the floor of the

cave, and each of them was introduced to the girl. She already knew Gopher and Owl, and had impressed them. That in turn impressed Indigo, because Owl was a surly bird not much given to socialization. If he thought there was something to this girl, there probably was. But it wasn't certain until they knew more about her. Too bad they didn't have their sixth member yet, a smart one, so that they could make swift and accurate judgments about such things. A burrow took on the mental ability of its most talented member, and that could make a significant difference. As it was, they had to gather for burrow meetings, and still not be certain their insights were correct.

"We must decide whether to maintain contact with this other realm," Gopher thought. As a tortoise he tended to be slow of thought, but fairly objective; when he came to a conclusion, it was usually correct. "Rowan Human Girl wants us to stay in touch. The other creatures of her realm do not have mental communication, so seem dull. But the humans are smart despite their lack of mind contact."

"This is hard to credit," Cottontail thought, leaping to an objection. "The girl has mind contact. She may be borrowing our intellect."

"No I don't have telepathy," the girl thought, making accompanying vocal noises exactly as Gopher had mentioned. That was an irritation, but not important at the moment. "I mean, I'm the only one, and it's all because of Gopher. He showed me how to do it. No one else in my world has it."

"How can we be sure of that?" Cottontail asked. "We have met no other animals here."

"I met another tortoise," Gopher thought. "He seemed to have no mind."

"I met several chickens," Owl thought. As a bird, he found it easy to get an overview and to gain perspective. "They also seemed to have no minds. They were not mental, and they were stupid. It is possible that I happened to encounter stupid ones, but it seems more likely that they were typical of this realm."

"What of other humans?" Peba asked, getting to a

significant point. The armadillo was a swift digger, and tended to seek the bottom of things.

"I encountered one," Gopher replied. "He had a strong mind, but could not project his thoughts at all."

"That was only one," Peba thought. "One tortoise, one flock of chickens, one human man. That is not enough to judge a realm by."

"Does it matter?" Owl asked. "The question is whether to maintain contact with this realm, whatever its nature." That was indeed perspective.

"Yes it matters," Peba thought, still delving for the deepest essence. "Stupid animals and smart humans is a serious inversion of the natural order. If this is the case throughout this realm, it is surely worth avoiding."

"And if there really is no mind projection here," Cottontail thought, jumping to an obvious conclusion, "communication is seriously limited. We should have trouble having a dialogue with any creature."

"Why should we *want* a dialogue?" Indigo demanded. It was his nature to slither between facts or issues to discover hidden aspects. "These creatures seem best left alone."

"But I want to keep talking with you," Rowan protested. "All of you. I can't do that if you go away."

Indigo considered her more carefully. She was human, which was unfortunate, but she could communicate, which redeemed her considerably. She was also a child, which made him want to avoid hurting her feelings. Young creatures needed to be nurtured, not rebuked. "I think we lack information to decide. We don't know enough about your realm."

"You can find out!" she thought emphatically. "I'll be happy to show you anything I can. Anything at all. There's a lot that's interesting here."

"Then perhaps Rowan should show Indigo," Gopher suggested, seeking a way to make all their viewpoints align. "Then he will have information, and can share it with the rest of us."

"I was not suggesting that," Indigo thought quickly. "I was merely bringing out a somewhat hidden point."

"A good one," Owl thought. "We can't make a sensible decision without full information."

"I'll do it!" Rowan thought. "Whatever you want to see!"

There was a general murmur of acceptance. The burrow mates found this reasonable. Indigo realized that he was committed despite his reservation.

He slithered toward the girl. "Put down an arm," he thought to her.

"I can pick you up," she thought.

"I prefer to make my own way."

"Oh—like Owl." She put down an arm.

Indigo resented the notion that he was like Owl; a snake was not at all like a bird. But he slithered across her hand and wrist, and on up to her shoulder. He looped twice around her neck, loosely, getting comfortable. "Now stand and walk."

"Okay." She straightened up. "Uh, when do we meet again? I mean, with the rest of you."

"I will return here when finished," Indigo told her. "I will join the others in the burrow and report."

"Oh. Sure," she agreed without enthusiasm. He realized that she had wanted to meet the others again. But that was not the point of this mission.

"We will meet again when we have a decision," Gopher thought as he and the others proceeded up the ramp and into the hole.

"Okay." But it was clear that this was less than the girl wanted.

"Why do you wish to associate with us?" Indigo asked as they made their way out of the cave.

"Because I'm lonely and being with you is like family," she replied. "I mean, with your minds—the moment I'm near you, I know you, and we can be friends."

"Family? Friends?"

She laughed, a human mannerism. "Like burrow mates. You're a group, and you get along so great, and I like being a part of it, even if it's only for a little while."

They emerged from the cave. Light shone down; they were in the sink hole Gopher and Owl had described. "I can make my own way here," Indigo thought.

"Okay." She put down her arm, and he uncoiled and slithered to the ground. "Gee—you're a big snake. You must be five feet long, and thick."

"As a species we are the largest of our region," Indigo agreed. "Not all species are of a size to become sapient." He slithered rapidly up the rocky slope.

She was scrambling up after him. "That's something I don't understand. I know sapient means smart, but how come it doesn't apply to all animals in your world?"

"We are not sure. It may be that a certain mass of body is required to enable mind communication without spoiling it. Lizards and mice have small sharp thoughts, while bears and humans have large dull thoughts. Insects and worms don't have intelligent thoughts, but some larger fish do."

"I'm human. How come I have smart thoughts?"

"We don't know. Your entire realm seems to be different. I am here to ascertain the extent of the differences, so we can decide whether to maintain the portal between realms." He crested the slope and looked around. "You are in drought."

"I guess so," she agreed, reaching the regular ground. "Lot of things drying up. They say this sinkhole is usually filled with water."

"Then the portal may be cut off when it rains."

"Gee, I hope not!"

But her hopes were not what counted. "The landscape seems normal. There are mice and insects and the smells of larger creatures. I need to explore some of the different aspects of this realm."

"I suppose I could take you into town. But you'd have to hide; it's not safe for a snake on the street."

"Town?"

She made a mental picture of a cluster of structures, with many humans between them. "A lot of people."

"We don't have that many humans in our realm, and they don't cluster beyond small breeding units. How can there be so many here?"

She made that odd laughing sound. "I guess we're

good at breeding. There are a lot of us. In fact, too many of us; we're running out of things."

"Take me to your town."

"Okay. I'll bike in on the trail." She put down her arm, and he slithered up to circle her neck again. "But you know, if anyone sees you like this, there'll be trouble. People don't wear snakes around here. In fact, if I weren't in touch with your mind, I'd be very nervous about this."

"But I need to be secure, and this is the way a human beast of burden normally carries me, if there is not a how-dah."

"Maybe I can put a shirt on over you," she thought. She had stopped making vocal noises while thinking, which was a relief.

The girl walked to the structure she thought of as a house, and found a light shirt. It covered Indigo without stifling him. Then she got a thing she called a bicycle, and rode on it, traveling much faster than before. Indigo realized that these humans were even stranger than the burrow mates had thought; there were endless odd things about them.

"This telepathy," the girl asked as she rode. "It really fascinates me. I mean, without it I'd never be wearing a big snake around my neck! I'm learning it some, but it doesn't work at all unless I'm with one of you telepathic creatures."

"That is because we can project as well as receive, while normal humans can only receive, dully. They are locked in near null state."

"Null state?"

"There are four general states of mind contact," Indigo explained. "With null, we neither send nor receive. With limited, we communicate between two minds, as you and I are doing now. Bears and alligators can do that, but they aren't fully sapient, so it doesn't mean much. With general, we commune as burrow mates, with all of us receiving the thoughts of all. And sometimes we use mind sharing, when one allows another to borrow his mind and senses for some purpose."

"Borrow a mind? How can you do that?"

"That is not easy to describe. We do it only when one mind has a quality or power the other lacks, and there is a need to use it. But it has to be limited."

"I don't think I understand. What quality or power do you lack, that you need from another mind?"

"Sometimes I need to see the lay of the land, so I can run down a rattlesnake that is threatening a burrow mate. Owl can see the land, but doesn't understand the ways of snakes as I do. So he can fly up and let me share his senses, and I can do a much better survey."

"That seems neat. But do you know how to fly? You could crash."

"That is why it is limited. I can't fly, so Owl must keep enough of his mind to stay in the air. But I can see a lot."

"That sure must be fun," Rowan thought wistfully.

Indigo looked through an opening where the girl's shirt buttoned, and saw the trail ahead. "That looks like stone."

"It's asphalt. It's—I guess it's sort of ground-up stone mixed with tar, and they pour it out and let it harden, and there it is, a great bike path."

"I don't understand poured stone or how you can move so fast with this thing under your feet."

"Maybe you could share my mind and see how it is."

Indigo considered. "I think not. Mind sharing should be used only when there is real need, not for mere curiosity."

"For me, curiosity is real need." But she continued moving.

They came to a much larger paved path. The girl stopped, waiting by its edge. Suddenly a huge thing charged along it, right toward them. Indigo recoiled, in the process choking Rowan, who fell to the side, the bicycle clattering down. The thing charged right past, missing them, so close Indigo felt a wind from its passage. He relaxed, so that the girl could breathe again.

"I regret that," he thought. "I will be more careful."

She understood, because their minds were in touch. "If you want to see the town, you'd better get used to traffic," Rowan gasped. "That was just a car."

"That was not a monster?"

"A car. We ride in them. Like bicycles, only they're larger and have motors. They stay on the road. No need to fear them."

"But something that size could tread me flat!"

She nodded. "I see what you mean. Animals do get squished when they're on the road where a car passes. You just have to stay out of the way. No problem; just stay with me and I'll stay out of the way."

Indigo realized that he did not properly understand the terrors of this realm. He had never imagined such a threat. It was clear that it was not a safe place for creatures like him to be. He would tell the burrow mates that when he returned. That would not please the human girl, but it had to be.

Rowan mounted her bicycle again and rode along the side of the road. Another huge thing charged from behind, but went right by without touching them. Indigo forced himself to relax; she did know what she was doing, scary as it was.

They came to a collection of the structures she called buildings. These started the same size as the one she lived in, but grew larger. The cars crowded the road, and frequently stopped and waited before moving on. There were flashing lights all around. The whole thing was dizzying.

Perhaps the most worrisome thing about it was that all of this was made by humans—the smart yet mentally closed humans of this realm. They were impossibly numerous, and had made this enormous collection of frightening things. Definitely no place for sensible animals to be.

Those humans were moving busily all around the town, each garbed in the strange materials of this realm. He got whiffs of what looked like fabric from plants or animal fur, but was actually some alien stuff. Worse, all of their minds were closed. How could such shut-in minds make all these huge buildings and cars? It wasn't natural!

"That unnatural stuff is called nylon, or rubber," Rowan thought. "We make clothing from all kinds of things, and of course we use metals and plastics a lot too."

"I have seen enough," Indigo told her. "It is time to return."

She turned her bicycle around and rode back out of town. "Pretty bad, huh?" she asked.

"Awful," he agreed.

"Now you can see why I want to be with you folk. We have material things here, but you have nice minds."

That made Indigo pause. He knew they should let the portal close, because this was no realm for their kind. But how could it be better for the girl? They would be cutting her off, and that was not kind.

"Now I understand," he agreed. But he did not know how to resolve this conflict.

They reached the path and cycled back through the forest. "So what will you tell the burrow mates?" she asked.

"That this is an awful realm we should not associate with."

"I was afraid of that. But you know, you don't have to come here. I mean, not to the town or on the roads. Just far enough so I can talk with you. That's all I ask—just to be with you. Because of your telepathy; I really like it."

He could understand that. He would be lost without the mind contact. But if they kept the portal open, was there a danger of the things of this realm intruding on the other? That would be awful.

Yet the girl was not awful. Indigo found himself liking her. He had never liked a human before, but he had never before met a human with a sapient mind. She did not deserve to be locked into this realm where she was the only one who could communicate mentally.

He could not answer her. Therefore he stalled. "I am not able to make a decision, and perhaps the burrow mates will have trouble too. You know more of this realm than I do. If you will let me share your mind to consider the problem, maybe I can assess the situation better."

"Sure! And I can start by showing you how the bicycle works. And anything else you want to know. How do I share my mind?"

"You must drop your natural barrier to intrusion. I will enter. It will feel like something slithering into your head. You must let it happen, though it may repel you. I will pool our thinking, drawing on your knowledge of the things of this realm, so that we have all the information. Perhaps that will lead to an insight."

"Can I keep riding, or should I stop?"

"It would be better to stop, for it would be a distraction. Remember, this must be with your cooperation; if you wish me to leave, you can push me out immediately."

"Will I be gone? I mean, unconscious or something?"

"No, you will be with me, sharing. There will be two of us in your mind, communicating as we do now. But I will not need to ask you for information; I will have it directly from your memory."

She steered the bicycle to a nearby tree and stopped. She got off it, leaned it against the trunk, and then sat down with her back to another tree. "I'm ready."

Indigo lifted his head up along her neck until his snout was touching her cheek. Closeness made it easier. He reached for her mind, and found her cooperating. She was not well experienced at mind contact, but had learned surprisingly rapidly. "Go this way," he thought, forming a mood of acceptance.

"Like this?" She mimicked the mood exactly.

"Yes." He projected his mind into hers, and suddenly he was there inside it.

It was like sudden sunshine after a storm. Indigo's mind expanded phenomenally, becoming enormously larger and stranger than it had been. He had never before experienced such a vast scope of intellect; the entire burrow did not match it. Now he understood how it was that the humans of this realm had been able to accomplish so much: they had minds so strong that they didn't need telepathy! They could figure things out without it. In fact they had other ways to communicate, speech and writing, and these were almost as effective as direct thoughts. Perhaps even more so, because the writing was cumulative— a term he had never encountered until this moment. It allowed the minds of the past to give their knowledge to those of the present.

And of course the bicycle. Now he fathomed it completely. It used wheels—another new concept—to roll along, tripling the efficiency—yet another concept—of the one who used it. All it needed was a firm path to roll along. And the cars: four wheels instead of two, with a motor: now he understood what that was. And the town, with its collected buildings. Everything was clear. This was a functioning human society, not awful, just different.

There was also something else. Rowan had a problem preying on her awareness, and it related to the burrow mates. "What is this?" he inquired, touching the section.

"Oh, I wasn't going to say anything about that."

"Yet it concerns us. We should know."

She sighed—another human mannerism, wherein a mental state was echoed by a vocal noise. "I suppose so. It's that I got in trouble after rescuing Gopher. I wasn't supposed to be out at night, and they did a bed check and caught me. Uncle and Aunt aren't used to kids; they say that if I do it again they'll send me off to boarding school."

Indigo picked up unpleasant intimations. "This is a threat?"

"A dire one. Not only would I hate it, it would keep me away from you burrow folk. I couldn't stand that."

"Then you must not do that again."

She nodded. "All too true."

But his expanded understanding of things was only part of his new awareness. These things hardly mattered. What was vital was the power of this mind. It was unlikely that there was any mind to match it anywhere in the home realm. Not among the animals, and certainly not among the humans. Only the linked minds of the powerful councils could rival it.

"How came you by this enormous intelligence?" he asked, awed.

"Gee, I'm not that smart! I'm just a typical regular girl. Sometimes I make Bs in school, and sometimes Ds. There're lots of people smarter than I am."

Indigo saw that it was true. Rowan's experience in school—new concept—showed that she was an average— new concept—creature of her type. *All* humans were immeasurably smarter than any animal of the home realm.

This was horrifying. But there was one overwhelming compensation: these humans could not share their thoughts directly. Rowan was the only one, perhaps because she had been desperately looking for an escape from her personal situation when Gopher had come upon her. She had opened her mind to him, and discovered thought contact, and quickly learned to use it herself. Perhaps her mind was different from others in its ability to receive thought, and the chance meeting with a mind creature had opened that avenue. She had become one of them.

"When I leave this mind sharing, I will understand little of this," Indigo thought. "I understand it now only because I am using your mind. But I believe my understanding is accurate."

"That's great," she thought. "But what *is* your understanding?"

"That we must maintain the portal, so as to remain in contact with you, alone of all your kind. Our burrow needs your mind."

She clapped her hands together, making a sound, and joy suffused her awareness and his. "Great! That's what I want. I'll help you any way I can. But you know, we'll have to figure out a way to stop that big construction project."

Construction project. Now he fathomed that threat, from her mind and memory. There was much she didn't know about it, but what she did know was bad. Big machines—that was the term for bicycles, cars, and other mechanical things—would come and fill in the sink hole, and the portal would be inaccessible. Perhaps Gopher could tunnel through somewhere else, but there would be more of the asphalt pavement in the way, too hard for him to get through. Also cars, which were very dangerous to tortoises and other animals. Bad all around.

"This is much more than I comprehend, even with your wonderful mind," Indigo thought. "We must have another burrow meeting to decide."

"I guess you're right. I sure don't know what to do."

"Now I will withdraw from your mind."

"Okay. But it's been fun being a big snake and slithering through things. I never thought to see one like you, let alone *be* one."

Indigo slithered out of her mind, and in a moment was himself, loosely coiled around the human girl's neck. The enormous comprehension was gone; now he had only ordinary understanding. But his conclusion was the same: they had to keep the portal open, and that would be a huge and dangerous mission. "We must return to the cave."

"Sure." Rowan got on her bicycle and pedaled along the path. The trees and brush passed by rapidly.

"We must show your mind to the burrow mates. We had no idea it was so powerful."

"You seem smart enough to me."

"That is because you interpret our thoughts with your big mind, and think we are equivalent. We are not. That is why we must pool our minds in burrow meetings. Five can think better than one. But you can think better than all of us together."

"But you can do the same things I do."

"No. You can stand and balance; I can lift my head only when braced. You can ride the bicycle; I could never do that, even if I had appendages. You can talk verbally, and read words with your eyes. I can't. You can understand complicated relationships. You can remember and use the past, and you can conceive the future. I have no such abilities."

"But you're talking about them right now!"

"I fathomed them when I was sharing your mind. Now I can evoke them just a little, because there is a trace of mind sharing when we communicate. But when I am away from you I will lose even the memory of their existence. They are only a few of the mental feats you can perform; I have no awareness of the others, except that I knew of them when I shared your mind."

"Oh, you mean like math? Politics? Art? Music? Verbs and nouns?"

"These are beyond my comprehension, whatever they are."

"I guess I understand, then. You can deal with me

one on one, but you're no artist or philosopher."

"That must be the case."

"So I guess you creatures aren't smart like humans, but you don't need to know square roots or the Mona Lisa painting to get along. You just need to know how to catch a mouse and find home. And how to get along with your burrow mates."

"Yes. The burrow gives us protection. When I sleep there, I know that no eagle will swoop down to clutch me. If I am hungry and hunting is bad, a burrow mate will tell me where there is prey. If I am injured, burrow mates will help me as much as they can. It is a good place to be."

"It's the telepathy. It gives you empathy. You can feel each other's feelings."

"Yes. A little when we communicate, a lot when we share minds. When we are together in the burrow, we know each other well, and that makes our sharing stronger. We can communicate at greater distance when we know each other well."

"That's what really gets me. If I saw a regular snake your size, I'd be wary, maybe scared. But with telepathy, I *know* you. And like you. You're friends."

"Now I understand your concept. Yes, we are friends. We will not do each other harm, though we are of different species. We are a group."

"I was so very much alone. Then Gopher came, and I had a friend. Maybe not really; maybe the telepathy just made it seem that way. But I liked him from the start. And Owl. And you. I want to be with you as much as I can. I'm never lonely with you."

"We will try to keep the portal open," Indigo promised. "I think the others will want to visit with you, if you will share your mind with them. It is an experience like no other."

"Sure. I've got the mind, you've got the telepathy. We've each got something the other wants, so we can share."

"We can share," Indigo agreed. "I no longer have trouble associating with a human on an equal basis. You are not at all like the others of our realm."

"Realm," she thought. "Now I understand that, from

when we shared. You're not from another world, but from another reality or something—like ours, only different. A world would be like a another planet, but you're on this planet, just another version. Where the animals are smart and the humans dull. Because of the telepathy. We had to get really really smart to make up for our lack of telepathy, like an electric car needing a lot of power to tote the heavy batteries along."

"I do not understand your analogy, but know you are correct."

"You could share my mind again, for the electric car."

"Would it help me function in life?"

She laughed, and now he understood that this was an expression of good-natured humor. Humor was a human concept, a pleasant one; it meant that something was nice in an odd way. "No, I don't think so. I guess my mind is too big; it runs off in directions that don't much matter."

"When I shared it, I understood the usefulness of such concepts. This makes me more tolerant of what I don't understand."

"Just so long as you aren't turned off."

"I am dismayed by your realm, but not by you."

Her surge of pleasure came right through her thought, making him feel good. "Thanks!"

They left the path and bumped across the field. The bicycle did not work as well where the ground was not hard and level. "This becomes uncomfortable," Indigo thought.

"I guess we'd better walk now. You can slither; we're close to the sinkhole." She stopped the bicycle, leaned down, and let him get to the ground.

It was good to travel on his own again. He slithered rapidly between tufts of dry grass while she walked behind him.

Rowan looked around. "There's someone out here."

"Another human?" The two of them were no longer in physical contact, but now they knew each other well enough so that there was no problem keeping mental contact.

"Two or three. One's got a pole. They must be surveyors."

Indigo did not understand that concept. "Can we avoid them?"

"Oh, sure. They're not paying any attention to us. I'm the only one they can see anyway."

She was correct: the humans did not come toward them. Soon they reached the brink of the sinkhole and descended to its bottom.

They entered the cave and went to the ramp and burrow hole. No one else was there. "I will inform the burrow mates," Indigo thought. "We will come here at noon tomorrow."

"I don't think we should wait," Rowan thought. "Those surveyors—they must be setting it up for the construction. Whatever we do, it needs to be fast."

"I will bring the burrow mates soon."

"I'll go back to the house for a bite to eat, and be back here within an hour." She reached down to touch Indigo, strengthening the concept.

"An hour," he agreed, now understanding the unit of time. Then he slithered up the ramp and into the hole.

"Bye," her thought came after him. It was a mood of parting.

"Bye," he echoed. He was picking up her foibles, ever since discovering her amazing mind.

Chapter 5
Quest

Cottontail heard the summons: something was happening at the burrow. He took a last munch of leaf and ran swiftly home. He saw Gopher doing the same. Gopher was closer to the burrow, but of course Cottontail got there ahead of him.

It turned out that Indigo was back from the other realm, and he was unusually excited. "The human girl has a mind bigger than all of ours together," the snake thought. "I think there is none like it in this realm. The rest of you must share with her to appreciate it."

Trust Indigo to slither into something no one else had thought of! But his mind showed it was true: he had shared with the girl, and discovered something amazing. They had been surprised when she turned out to be sapient, but it seemed that her limited telepathy had masked the true power of her huge brain. Indigo, who had been cool to the idea of maintaining the portal between realms, now was firmly in favor of it. That was persuasive.

"But she has a problem," Indigo continued. "Her burrow threatens to expel her because she went foraging at night."

"But many creatures forage at night!" Cottontail protested. He preferred day, but Owl and Peba liked night.

Indigo clarified that he lacked the proper concept. Rowan Girl had gone with Owl to rescue Gopher, and her burrow mates objected. She was not supposed to be out at night.

"I had not understood that," Owl thought.

"Neither had I," Gopher agreed. "I never thought to have her suffer for my sake."

"She did for you what a burrow mate would do," Cottontail thought. "But she is not a burrow mate."

That made them all pause. It complicated the discovery of the power of her mind. Why would a creature outside the burrow do such a thing?

They considered. "We must each share her mind, to understand," Gopher thought. "Then we can decide."

"We must go immediately," Indigo thought. "I told her we would."

It was obvious that the snake had experienced something that had truly impressed him. That made Cottontail curious. Gopher and Owl had been with the girl before, and were in favor; they both liked her. Now Indigo liked her too. So it was time to find out just what it was about her mind that made a lowly human worth so much trouble.

They moved down the tunnel in rapid single file, Indigo leading, Cottontail next. Gopher was their slowest member, so he trailed, but remained in thought contact.

Indigo and Cottontail came to the cave first and almost tumbled down the ramp. There was the human girl, just arriving. "You came!" she thought gladly. The others were right: there was something pleasant about her despite her humanity.

"We are all coming," Indigo thought. "Will you share you mind with all of us?"

"Sure." She looked at Cottontail. "You're just the cutest bunny! May I pick you up and cuddle you?"

Flattered by her interest, Cottontail agreed. She reached down, put her two hands about his body, and lifted him to her chest. That close, it was easy for him to share her willing mind.

It was like entering a lush garden of delicious plants. His awareness expanded beyond all bounds. Suddenly he understood the cave, the realm, and everything in a way never fathomed before. A burrow gathering enhanced the smartness of all of them, for they shared their resources, but this was like a burrow of hundreds! Every thought led to a labyrinth of understanding, like a path through that garden, and every path seemed more wonderful than any other. He was not the smartest creature of his realm, but this made him so.

Then Peba Armadillo joined him. "This is deeper than I have ever delved," he thought. "I never realized that such intellect was possible. There are grubs here I never dreamed of."

The girl laughed, and they understood her humor. "Grubs! Suddenly they make my mouth water." It seemed that she did not normally eat grubs, but the sharing gave her Peba's appreciation for them. It also gave cottontail and Peba appreciation for thought so complicated that it became an end in itself. Rowan had memories extending back before the burrow mates had existed, and understood how to play games that would have been not only incomprehensible but pointless to any of the burrow mates when apart from her. Yet she was a child, not yet in full possession of her abilities. This was truly amazing.

Indigo joined them in sharing. "Now you appreciate why we must keep the portal open. We must retain contact with Rowan Girl, alone of all in her dangerous realm."

Indeed they did. This girl was a lot more interesting than any of them had supposed when they first learned of her.

"But we do not want any others of her realm to learn mind contact—telepathy," Peba thought. "With minds that powerful, they would be dangerous to us."

"They sure would!" Rowan agreed. "Telepathy gives you community; we need big brains to make up for our close-mindedness. But if we had telepathy too, there'd be no stopping us. We're—we're not all nice people."

Now they were all there, sharing her mind, holding a burrow meeting outside the burrow.

"But what is this problem with your burrow?" Cottontail inquired.

"Oh, that! It's not my burrow, it's just my relatives.

My uncle and aunt, who are boarding me while my folks back home sort things out. They don't much understand children, and I don't much understand them. We mostly ignore each other. That's one reason I was so intolerably lonely."

Yet they had set a limit on her, and she would suffer mischief if she failed to honor it.

"It would be safer to let the portal close," Peba thought.

"You're right," Rowan agreed. "It's selfish of me to want to keep it open. We should let it be sealed off." They could feel the sadness in her; she was trying to do the right thing. That was another new concept: that things could be right or wrong, rather than just there.

"Not after we have shared your mind," Indigo thought. "We have to share more of it."

There was agreement from the others. They reveled—(new concept)—in the powers of her mind; it was addictive—(new concept)—and they couldn't let it go.

"Addiction is dangerous," Rowan thought. She expanded the concept.

But in a moment they realized that what was addictive wasn't always addiction. The experience of her mind was new and wonderful to them, but they were not locked into it. It was merely a great pleasure of association.

"That's a relief," Rowan thought.

"We will keep the portal open," Gopher thought, deciding for all of them. "How can we do that?"

"We must explore," Cottontail thought. "We must find out how to stop the other humans from closing it."

"Do it," Peba thought, and there was agreement.

Before he knew it, Cottontail found himself outside the cave with Rowan. She set him down in the sinkhole, and he bounded up its slope to the top, eager to explore this realm. He crested the rim.

Something pounced on him. He was bowled over. He tried to scramble to his feet, but the thing was on him, grabbing his foot with its teeth.

"Cottontail!" Rowan shrieked. "It's a cat! A feral cat!"

A cat—and its mind was closed. Cottontail couldn't divert it with a mental image. The thing was going to consume him!

"Get away from him, cat!" Rowan cried. Cottontail realized that though the cat was mind-closed, it could hear the vocal sounds she was making. It hesitated.

But then it bit his foot again. The pain flared.

"Stop it!" Rowan screamed. She picked up a stone and hurled it. The stone struck the cat's flank, making it snarl and whirl.

Cottontail tried to scramble away, but the cat whirled again and caught him. Rowan threw another stone. Then she crested the rim, and swept up a stick. She beat the cat on the back. It snarled again, but retreated. Rowan picked Cottontail up. The cat, seeing the issue had become hopeless, turned and ran away.

"I'm so sorry," Rowan said, cuddling Cottontail. "I didn't know that cat was there. I never would have set you down if I had known! Are you all right?"

He was not all right. His foot had been bitten twice and was mangled. It hurt horribly. He would have to run three-legged.

"Oh, I wish this hadn't happened," Rowan wailed. "That darned cat!" Then she focused on him. "I've got to get you to the house. We have pain-killing ointment, bandages—"

"I don't want any of that," Cottontail protested. "I don't understand it. I need to get home to the burrow, and another burrow mate can come to help you search."

"But they won't be at the cave now, and you can't run up that tunnel slope with that bad paw."

She was right. But he still didn't want to get into treatments he didn't understand. "I will use the foot as it is, if I can suppress the pain."

"You can do that? Stop the pain?"

"In the burrow we can do it. The burrow mates focus together, sharing minds, and make it go away."

"Maybe I can help, then. I'll share my mind. But you'll have to tell me how to dampen the pain."

Maybe it would work; she had a powerful mind.

They shared minds. Again he felt the expanding wonder of her intelligence making him smarter than any rabbit had ever been. "Now focus on making the pain fade," he thought.

She focused. Her awareness centered on his hurting foot, surrounding it. The pain faded almost immediately. It just couldn't stand up to that concentration.

"It's gone," she thought. "I feel it! Your foot feels better." Then she reconsidered. "But it isn't really better. We damped out the pain, that's all; you can't use it. But I can carry you, and we'll got the job done."

"I should never have been so careless," Cottontail thought ruefully. "I was fooled by the lack of a mind trace, and thought no predator was near."

"This is the realm of closed minds," she agreed. "That makes it dangerous." She looked around. "The surveyors are closer now. They must be zeroing in on this sinkhole to know exactly what it will take to fill it in. We may not have much time."

"They will fill it in?"

"No, the big company that wants to build the mall will do that. But maybe the surveyors know who is the big boss."

The girl carried him toward the human men. "You must hide me," Cottontail thought.

She considered. "I don't see how I can, unless I put you in my shirt the way I did Indigo. But you can't hang on the way he did; it would look funny. I think I'd better just carry you; I'll tell them you're my pet bunny. They'll never suspect your real nature."

Cottontail wasn't easy about this, but there seemed to be no good alternative. He did not want to risk the ground again; that mindless cat might still be near.

They came to the man holding the pole. He was young, Rowan's mind thought, maybe twenty years old, and halfway handsome. Physical appearance was important to the humans of this realm. "Hi!" Rowan called.

The man nodded acknowledgment. That was a human trait; in both realms they had many physical signals, because of their lack of telepathy. "Hi. Got your pet bunny along?"

"Yes. His foot got chomped." She indicated the injured foot.

"Too bad. But I guess you'll take good care of him."

"I sure will. Whatcha doing?"

"I'm surveying," the man answered, halfway flattered to be asked. His mind was mostly closed, but a bit of that thought came through. Cottontail realized that the man was transmitting the message vocally, and the girl was understanding it in her head as thoughts. Cottontail was reading those thoughts in her mind. It was an unusual way to communicate, but this was an unusual realm.

The girl flashed the man an innocent smile. Cottontail found that instructive: she was consciously pretending to be the child she was. That seemed to make sense at the moment. "How does that work?"

"It's for the traverse," he said, with her mind translating his vocals. "That is, well, the man with the theodolite—" He paused because of her blank look. "He sights on this pole, getting the azimuth—the direction—and then we measure from there to here, and—well, we're just getting an exact notion where things are. That's what surveying is."

"Gee," she said, putting on big eyes. It was in her mind: children were supposed to have big eyes. It made them look innocent. "Why are you doing it?"

"We're on assignment for this big outfit, MDI. We do what they tell us, because they pay our way."

"MDI?"

"Mall Development Inc. Biggest outfit in these parts. They're going to put a huge mall here."

"Gee. The guy who runs that must be pretty important."

"He sure is. That's Mr. Bennington. I hear he's coming up here tomorrow to see how it's going. So we mean to have the survey done right."

"Guess I'd better get out of your way, then. Bye."

"Bye," he agreed as she walked away.

"You found the key person," Cottontail thought.

She nodded. "Mr. Bennington," she thought, keeping her mouth closed. "He's the one we have to reach."

"You have an idea," Cottontail thought, feeling it in

her mind.

"Yes. Maybe if we can just talk to Mr. Bennington, we can get him to stop the construction. Or at least do it somewhere else."

"Why would he do that?"

"Gee, I hadn't thought that far. He's not going to change his mind just because a ten-year-old girl asks him to, and I can't ask him anyway, because then he'd want to know why, and I can't tell him. I can't tell anybody in this realm. So I guess it's a bad idea."

Cottontail considered. He found it easy to be thoughtful, because of his contact with her large mind. "The burrow mates might have a better idea. But I can't just bound back to them while my foot is injured. We'll have to get a better idea ourselves."

"We can try," she agreed. "Maybe if we knew exactly why he's putting the mall here, we could find a reason to put it somewhere else."

"Can we guess?"

"Sure. Malls are big shopping centers. They put them in cities, or where there are several towns close by, so a lot of people will come. They must figure people will come here, and they'll make a lot of money."

"Money?"

"I guess you don't have it in your realm. It's a—a way of getting things without working for them right then. Everybody wants more money."

"Could we find some money for him so he wouldn't need it from the mall?"

She shook her head. "I don't think so. It's not easy to find money."

"Could there be something else he wants, that we could find for him?"

She laughed. "Not telepathy! That's out, even if he has the mind for it. But maybe we should study his mind, if we can. Just in case there's something. We're desperate."

Cottontail agreed. "We can learn about him today, and go to see him tomorrow. I think I will have to go to your home this night."

"I agree. You need to let that foot heal, so you can run up the tunnel to your burrow. I can scrounge up some lettuce for you, or whatever."

She carried him to the house she lived in, and she hid him in her room. She brought him assorted types of food, such as lettuce, bread, and a carrot. They were not his normal diet, but edible.

She also fetched a pile of papers she called a newspaper. There was what she called an article that confirmed that Mr. Bennington, the CEO of MDI, the mall maker, was in town. "Tomorrow," she thought with excitement. "Tomorrow we can go see him. Maybe it'll be all right."

✍ ✎

Next morning after eating and seeing the adults go out, Rowan packed a traveling bag with a pretty red dress and matching shoes. "These are my company clothes," she explained to Cottontail. "For when I have to be a Girl. I hardly ever use them. But if I'm to talk with this big old boss man, I'd better play the part."

"Why don't you like being a girl?" Cottontail asked.

"My mother was a girl. Then she grew up and got married and became a drudge. I don't want any of that. I'd rather play computer games, and run through fields of flowers forever. But I know I'll grow up all too soon anyway."

"I am a young rabbit. I am eager to grow up. All of the burrow mates are young. We all want to grow up and complete the burrow and be recognized."

"Well, you have a better realm," she thought. "I'd surely want to grow up too, if I could be a citizen there."

That did seem to make sense. The girl's mental picture of grown life was grim. It seemed that humans worked all day, just as the ones of this house did, and seldom relaxed.

She carried him and the bag down to her bicycle. "You can ride in one pannier and I'll jam the bag in the other. But I'm not sure what we'll do in town."

"I do not think it would be safe for me to run on the ground, even if my foot were better," he thought. "You will have to carry me."

"Right. But how will I carry you so as not to make a scene?"

"In the bag."

"But there's not room for you along with my clothing." Then immediately she answered her own objection. "The jeans can stay with the bike. Got it."

They rode into town. This was a new experience for cottontail, but her mind reassured him. He hunched down in the pannier, peeping out through crevices in the material.

The first stop was at the library. "I can check the newspaper file here, and change in their rest room," she thought.

She removed the dress and put Cottontail in the bag. Then she carried both into the building. She went to the front desk. "I understand Mr. Bennington is in town today," she thought with vocals to the woman she thought of as the librarian. "I'd like to look at recent newspaper clippings on him."

"We have online access," the librarian vocalized, the translated thoughts coming through Rowan's mind. "I'll set it up for you."

"Great!" Her thought continued: "I forgot that a library would have a computer. This makes it much easier."

"What is that?" Cottontail asked.

"Its a—a machine that lets you connect all over the world. Like—well, suppose you had an animal who could reach out its mind to anyone in your realm, no matter how far away? This is sort of like that. Only it's limited to a screen. Just follow my mind as I research; you'll see."

The bicycle was a machine that helped the girl travel. It seemed this was another kind of help. The wonders of this realm just kept coming.

Soon Rowan was looking into a machine, deep in research about the man. It turned out that the obscure markings on the screen spoke to her mind; she called this Reading, and it was much the same as the vocal sounds. It was as if Cottontail was receiving thoughts from the screen, all about this important man. "He's got a granddaughter my age!" she exclaimed. "That's great! He'll be a soft touch for a winsome girl." She grimaced. "Though I *hate* being winsome."

She went to the rest room and quickly changed clothing. She donned the pretty dress, put on the matching shoes, combed out her hair, and tied it back in a loose ponytail with the ribbon. Cottontail followed all this in her mind with interest; she was making herself into a Girl.

Rowan carried the bag and her old clothing out of the library. She put them into the pannier baskets and mounted the machine. "I don't like dressing like this," she thought. "And I *really* don't like riding a bike in a dress! But it has to be done."

"Your kind is much influenced by appearance," Cottontail thought, trying to understand.

"Yes—especially when it comes to girls. It's even worse with big girls. I hate it, but that's the way it is."

They came to another building. "This is the hotel where Mr. Bennington is staying," Rowan explained. "Now comes the hard part."

Cottontail felt her nervousness. "Is this thing dangerous?"

"In a way. If it doesn't work, I may be in trouble. Again."

She took the bag with Cottontail, leaving her other clothing in the basket. She entered the building.

"This is where the man is?" Cottontail asked.

"It's his hotel. It's time for lunch, so I figure he'll eat here. He has business in the afternoon, so he has to eat now. If I guessed right."

"What if you guessed wrong?"

"That's another kind of trouble. I won't catch him, and we won't be able to talk him out of the project. So I've *got* to catch him."

"Maybe I can help. I can seek his mind."

"But you don't know him. How can you find his mind? Especially if it's closed?"

"There may be some leakage. I can search for thought about the big mall project."

"Okay. See if you can tell whether he's here?"

Cottontail searched, and soon found thoughts of the

mall. It was easier, because most minds here were closed, so there was little mental clutter; he was able to orient on that single thought. "Yes, he is in this building."

"Great! What direction?"

He showed her mind the direction.

"That's where the hotel restaurant is. So I guessed right."

She came to the restaurant. But as she was going in, a man intercepted her. Cotton felt her thrill of alarm.

"May I help you miss?" the words came, phrased as a question, but it was actually a challenge. Cottontail felt her mixed reactions as she figured out how to respond.

"I—I was looking for someone," she answered the man, who it seemed was a hotel official, somewhat like the burrow landlord. "I don't know whether he's here yet."

"Who?"

"Mister—Mister Bennington."

"Yes, he is having lunch. However—"

"Good!" She slid by him and went into the restaurant.

"Hey!" But he did not pursue her.

"Now where *is* he?" she thought desperately. There were several men at tables, and none matched the picture in the newspaper file.

"I pick up a mind trace of a business person," Cottontail thought. "I believe it is the same one that thought of the mall before. That way." He indicated the direction with a mental nudge. Because he was in the bag, he could not see directly, and was focusing on mental things.

"You're sure? I don't want to barge in on the wrong person." Her nervousness continued. Cottontail was aware of her pulses racing.

"It is the only one of its kind," he assured her.

"Okay. I'm taking the plunge." She headed in that direction.

Rowan found Mr. Bennington's table. He was alone, sipping a glass of something. "Now it's do or die, or maybe both," she thought. "I just hope my nerve holds out."

"I can support that." Cottontail sent a bolstering signal, supporting her confidence.

"Hey, I feel that! Thanks!"

She slid into the chair opposite the man. She smiled as he looked up, startled.

"Are you lost, child?" Mr. Bennington asked.

"I hope not," Rowan said, smiling again. "You're the important Mr. Bennington, aren't you?"

"I am Mr. Bennington, but I don't believe I know you."

"I'm Rowan." She smiled once more. Cottontail was aware of the effort it took; she was frightened.

"Oh—you must be a friend of my granddaughter's. She's not with me today."

"Mr. Bennington, I don't know your granddaughter. But I wish I did. She must be a nice girl."

Cottontail felt the man focusing suspiciously. "What are you doing here?"

"Mr. Bennington, please don't be mad at me. I just *had* to talk to you."

The suspicion remained. "What possible business could a girl like you have with me?"

"The big mall. I live right near it, and where I play is going to be all paved over. Please, please, Mr. Bennington, don't build it there!"

"Child, to you have any idea how much is invested in this project? We can't simply—"

"I hate this," Rowan thought to Cottontail as she clouded up her face, forcing tears.

It worked. Cottontail felt the emotion. Rowan reminded the man of his granddaughter, and he did not like to see her cry. Cottontail reached out with his thought, reinforcing that mood. It was not easy to get into the man's mind, but it was possible to enhance naturally occurring thoughts. "Oh, please, child! There are other places for you to play. I'm sure your family will be amply compensated for its property."

"But—but it won't be the same! They're going to fill in the big sinkhole!" She dabbed at her face with a tissue.

The man in charge of the restaurant approached. Cottontail felt his mind: he had decided that the girl was an intruder and needed to be removed. "Is this person bothering you, Mr. Bennington?"

Bennington man opened his mouth to speak. Rowan gave him a tearful look. He hesitated. Cottontail felt the interplay of the three human minds, and gave another shove in the right direction. "Er, no, thank you, maitre d'. It's quite all right."

Not fully reassured, the man retreated.

"Thanks for not turning me in," Rowan said. She made a hesitant smile, like a trace of sunshine peeking around a cloud.

"Child, that doesn't change the situation. Actually I don't even decide exactly where the mall will be located; there are two promising sites, and the better one will be selected in due course." But now the man wanted the girl to like him. He knew she was not his granddaughter, but the emotional association was strong. Cottontail was making sure of that.

"Two sites," Rowan repeated. "Who does decide?"

"My leading consultant, George Dayson of Dayson Consultancies. His judgment is unerring, and I have learned to defer to it. He is even now in the final stage of evaluation, and I expect his report within days. So perhaps your concern is not merited."

"Dayson," she repeated, memorizing it. "You do what he says."

"In a manner. Of course the final responsibility is mine, but as I said—"

"Thanks, Mr. Bennington. I'll go talk to him." She stood up.

But the association, once enhanced, was not readily stopped. "Now wait, child! It is hardly that simple."

Rowan froze in place. "It isn't?"

Mr. Bennington smiled. "Stay and visit with me, and I will explain. You do remind me of my granddaughter."

"I—I really can't—"

"Ice cream? What flavor?"

Cottontail felt the surge of longing. She did like ice cream. "I don't—I shouldn't—"

Mr. Bennington caught the maitre d's eye, and suddenly the man was at the table. "A dish of your finest ice cream for my friend. Chocolate, I think."

Cottontail felt the girl's temptation. She believed she shouldn't stay, but she longed for that ice cream. The man was very good at managing people. "Mr. Bennington, you don't owe me anything! I just came to talk to you."

The man nodded to the maitre d'. "Fetch it." Then, to Rowan: "I understand that. And I told you whom to contact. Now you must pay for that information."

"Pay?" she asked blankly.

"Information is as valuable as substance. You owe me."

"But—"

"One visit. Stay and chat until you're done with your ice cream. Then you are through."

Cottontail saw that the man truly missed his granddaughter, whom he seldom saw, and wanted the company of a girl like her. "Do it," he urged Rowan.

She yielded. "Okay."

The ice cream arrived at the same time as the man's main course, so they ate together. The ice cream was really good, the best she had ever tasted; Mr. Bennington truly had ordered the finest. They chatted amicably about this and that, and it was surprisingly pleasant. "He's a nice man," she thought to Cottontail. "I thought he'd be horrible."

Cottontail knew that the man was neither nice nor horrible; he simple worked to get what he wanted, whether that was a big mall or the brief attention of a girl who reminded him of his absent granddaughter. But there seemed to be no harm in this association, and he felt the pleasure of the ice cream. It made him hungry for a green garden; it had been long since he had eaten.

"Why do you wish to save that particular sinkhole?" Mr. Bennington asked.

"You can't tell him the truth," Cottontail thought.

"I know." Then she spoke aloud. "It's where I play. There are rabbits there, and tortoises."

"We are relocating the tortoises."

"I know. But I don't want them to be ripped from their homes the way I was."

The man gazed at her a moment with a certain understanding. More of his mind was coming through; he was eerily smart. Then he shifted the subject somewhat. "You don't wish there to be a tort for your tortoises."

"Tort?"

"That is a wrongful act, not a breach of contract, that results in injury to another person. You feel the mall would harm your tortoises, so you seek redress."

"That's it!" she exclaimed. "Tort reform!"

He smiled. "The legal concept is not quite what you may believe. But it will do for a pun: tortoise reform."

"I guess." The thought of Gopher being reformed made her smile.

Mr. Bennington clarified the concept of tort reform, but it was well beyond Cottontail's power to comprehend. It was something about limiting the liability of corporations. Cottontail let that be and concentrated on maintaining the connection between Rowan and the man.

In due course, as Rowan was finishing her ice cream, the man's cell phone beeped. "I don't want to eavesdrop," Rowan said quickly, standing. Mr. Bennington nodded as he brought out the phone and answered. He was a businessman, and this was business.

"That turned out to be fun," Rowan thought as they returned to her bicycle. "And it's a lesson to me not to pre-judge people. I really had that man figured wrong."

"I enhanced his feeling for you," Cottontail explained. "But then I couldn't turn it off."

"Oho! So that why he got so friendly after I barged in! I should have known. But how could you do it, if he's not telepathic?"

"I could read some of his mind, because I was close and his thoughts were strong, and I could strengthen his feeling. That was all."

"So it is possible to get into the minds of humans, a little. I can't do it, but you can."

"You are learning. You tried to make of him think of his granddaughter by the way you dressed, but you did it a little with your mind as well. The two of us together made it work."

They reached the bicycle. "Now let me got back into

decent clothing, and we'll go home." She lifted the other clothing out of the basket and looked around. "But where can I change?"

"You can't do it here?"

"Someone might see me in my underwear."

Cottontail learned from her mind that it was not good for a human person to be seen by others without clothing. "Could you change here if no one saw you?"

"Sure. But someone could come along at any time."

"You can hide in a crevice, and I will extend my awareness and warn you if any humans come near."

She considered a moment, then agreed. "This is nervy, but not worse that approaching Mr. Bennington was." She carried the clothing and Cottontail to an alcove by a building. "Is the coast clear?" Her mind showed a picture of a sea shore, but also what she meant: that no one was near.

Cottontail expanded his awareness. "There is no one close."

"Okay." Rowan struggled quickly out of her shoes and dress, and into her jeans and shirt.

"A human female is approaching," Cottontail warned.

She ripped the ribbon from her hair and wadded the dress into a ball. Then she walked back to the bicycle. A woman walked by, not paying any attention to the girl. Rowan put the clothing into one basket, and Cottontail's bag into the other, and got on the bicycle.

"Gee, that was fun!" she exclaimed. "I was really scared someone would see."

"You enjoy being frightened?"

"Yes, if it's not too bad. You were alert, so I knew it was okay, but it still *seemed* dangerous. That's why it's fun."

Cottontail considered that. "I think I understand, but I will not understand when I am no longer in contact with your mind."

"I guess rabbits can't afford to play at danger; there's too much real danger for them."

"Yes. We are safe only in the burrow."

"We'll get you back there soon."

She was correct. First they returned to the library,

where Rowan did spot research on George Dayson of Dayson Consultancies. She learned that he lived in Horseman's Estate, a big development north of the big city. She noted the address. After that she rode the bicycle to the sinkhole and then carried the bag down into it. The survey men were not there this day, so they had no concern about discovery.

They entered the cave and reached the burrow tunnel. No one was there, but that could be fixed. Cottontail sent a thought out to intercept Gopher.

Gopher answered. "Cottontail's back!" he thought to the others. "But he is injured. We must go there."

"They will come," Cottontail thought.

"It's been great being with you," she thought. "I'm sorry you got injured."

"I was careless. Had you not saved me, I would have been eaten."

"That would have been awful! At least now we know who we have to talk to, to move the mall."

Cottontail leaped to a conclusion. "Not talk, or think. We have to change his mind. That will require all of us, working together."

"All of you!"

Then the burrow mates started arriving.

Chapter 6
Mission

Peba Armadillo could move rapidly when he wanted to, and his alcove was the deepest in the burrow, so when Gopher's call came, he was the first to reach the deep cave. Cottontail was there, of course, and so was the human girl.

"How did you get hurt?" he asked.

"I was careless. A cat pounced on me. Rowan saved me, but I can run only with pain."

Cats were not much of a threat to Peba, but he felt Cottontail's pain. "Then you must rest. We will fetch you plants to eat."

"No. We must act immediately. Tonight, I think. There is a human who decides where the mall is put. We must change his mind."

The others were arriving, and they were already sharing minds. Soon they gathered around the human girl and considered. From that consideration came the conclusion: "Cottontail is correct," Gopher thought. "We must all go to change this human man's mind. It will not be receptive the way Rowan's mind is, so it will require more power than any one of us possesses."

"I wish I could help," Rowan thought. "But I can't do telepathy on my own. Just when one of you helps me."

"But you are learning," Cottontail thought. "In time you will be able to do it by yourself."

"I'd love that! But first things first: how do we organize to change that man's mind? I mean, he's not close by; I'm not sure how we can even get there."

"Your bicycle," Cottontail thought.

"That's no good for this. First, I don't know the way, and second the bike has no lights so I couldn't ride it at night, and it may be too far anyway. Third, I'd get picked up if the police saw me on the road at night. And how would I ever take all of you along? I might carry you, but not on the bike."

Peba delved to the root of the problem. "We all need to go, but you can't take us on your pedal machine. Is there another way?"

"Car, of course. I could put you all in a suitcase and tote you along; you'd be heavy, but I could do it. But I can't drive a car."

"And you can't go out at night," Indigo reminded her. "Your burrow forbids it."

She shook her head. "I've got to. It's the only way to save the portal. If we don't save it, there's not much point of my existence anyway." But the fear of that transgression came through; she was not comfortable with this.

"We need more information, for an overview," Owl thought. "We must explore your mind."

"Welcome to my mind," Rowan thought. "You like sharing it; I like sharing it with you. I never felt really brainy before, or beautiful the way you see me."

They joined her mind again, and again there was that sensation of enormous expansion as they all became far more intelligent than they had ever been. In a moment Indigo slithered to the key aspect: "You have a neighbor who uses a car at night."

"Oh, sure. That's Mr. Klondike, who works nights at the truck stop in Tangletree. He drives in after dark, and returns before dawn, so we hardly ever see him."

"Could we ride with him?" Cottontail asked. Peba knew that the rabbit did not want to run anywhere, with his painful foot.

"My folks wouldn't let me. Even if I weren't already in trouble for the last time I snuck out at night, to get Gopher."

"Is it needful to ask?" Peba asked, again getting to the bottom of it.

"Oh, my." Rowan pushed her hands through the hair of her head. "I guess I'm sort of in denial. We do have to get this done, and it had better be soon. All right, I'll sneak out tonight and get aboard Mr. Klondike's pickup truck. If he catches me I'm a goner, but maybe he won't check."

"We can discourage him from checking," Cottontail thought.

"But can you discourage my folks from checking my room at night, while I'm gone?"

There was general agreement: they could not influence any humans when they were not close by. Peba was not the only one who was not easy with this. They were asking a lot of the girl, and would also be risking themselves.

"I guess we'll just have to gamble," Rowan decided. "This scares me worse than broaching Mr. Bennington did. But maybe we can do it, because we could catch a truck going south in Tangletree and reach Horseman's Estate pretty soon. But this whole thing is so fraught with risk—I mean, I'm just a local girl, they'd just think I was running away or something, but you folk—if you got caught away from the cave, or worse, if they caught on to your nature—that would be disaster."

Peba felt her genuine fear, and knew it was justified. This was a dangerous business. But they considered, using the superior power of her mind, and concluded that it was a calculated risk—(new concept)—if they failed, they could all be in great danger, but if they succeeded, the portal would remain open, and they would be able to commune with Rowan whenever they wanted.

At last Gopher thought the consensus: they would do it. Because they were sharing Rowan's human mind, she was part of it: she wanted to gamble—(new concept)—too. All or nothing.

They all shared her fright, but also her determination.

"Okay, then," she thought weakly. "We'd better all go

home and get some rest, and I'll sneak out and come here to fetch you after dark. If I can find my way without using a light."

"I can find my way in the darkness," Peba thought. "My vision is not good, but it is almost as sharp at night as in light. I will go with you and guide you."

"And that will give me some telepathy, so I'll know how to avoid Uncle and Aunt," she agreed gladly. "Good enough; I fell less worse already."

They withdrew from her mind. Peba led the way out of the cave, while the burrow mates went up the tunnel to the burrow. The others were helping Cottontail suppress the pain of his foot so that he could limp up with them. Gradually their mind traces faded.

They entered the big sinkhole. "This is delightful!" Peba thought. "There are all manner of bugs in this ground."

"Eat your fill, because I sure don't want to dig them out for you," Rowan thought. "I never associated with an armadillo before. They don't live where I came from."

Peba followed his nose, sniffing out all manner of delicious incidentals. Then he crested the rim—and something pounced on him. It was the cat; he had been careless, just as Cottontail had.

But he was no soft bunny. He snapped into a ball, protecting his head and feet, and the cat was unable to hurt him. It should have known better than to go after an armored creature. His armor was not yet completely hard, because he was not yet full grown, but it was tough enough for this.

But the creature persisted, batting at his surface, trying to pry him open. This was annoying. "Lend me your mind," he thought to Rowan.

The girl did. They shared. Peba drew from her mind, and hurled a blast of savagery at the cat. The cat screeched and fled, not knowing what had hit it.

"Wow! Like a rock on the noggin. Serves it right," Rowan said, pleased. "I didn't know you folk could do that."

"By myself, I could not," Peba thought. "With the support of the burrow, I could. The cat's mind was closed, but orienting on me, so there was an opening. Your mind is so big, it's as good as the burrow, so I struck back. That was a pleasure."

They moved on. Peba ran along the ground while Rowan lifted her bicycle and walked beside it. "Getting into the mind of this key man tonight—I don't think stunning him will help."

"It would be too hard to affect a human mind that way," Peba thought. "We hope just to change it a little, using the method by which we normally direct humans in our realm."

"Oh, yes, I forgot—humans are beasts of burden where you are. But I guess their minds are more open."

"They are, because they have been trained to be responsive to sapient commands, and they are much weaker than yours. That is why we need to have all of us present for the effort. Cottontail showed that we could influence human minds of this realm, but only in a limited manner. We shall have to try very hard, and be very careful."

"I'll bet!"

Peba was keeping pace with her, but as they approached her house, Rowan had a concern for him. "If they see you, they may try to catch you or kill you," she thought. "People don't like wild creatures around the house; they are afraid they are going to do some damage. I'd better hide you."

"Hide me," Peba agreed.

"I'll put you in the basket and cover you with my dress."

She did that, then walked the bicycle on to the house. "Wow—you weigh more than Cottontail."

"Rabbits are at the low edge of size for full sapience, just as wildcats are at the high edge. Armadillos are in the middle."

"Some time I really want to understand more about that sapient range. But right now I'd better focus on this job." Then she parked the bicycle in the shed, wrapped Peba in the dress, and carried him into the house. She unwrapped him in her room. "I'll bring you some—can you eat green leaves the way Cottontail does?"

"Can you find me some buggy ones?"

She laughed. "I'll ransack the garbage."

Peba snoozed while she went to supper with the family. She did bring him some buggy fruit that had been thrown out; it was delicious.

Later that night, when Peba's expanded awareness indicated that the relatives were not paying attention, Rowan packed two traveling bags with crumpled paper and put Peba in one. "If they catch me with these, they'll think I'm running away," she thought. "So I'd better not get caught." She also set up her bed so that it looked as if a person was sleeping in it. "I sure hope they don't do a competent bed check!"

Then they sneaked out. This was another new concept for Peba, for in the burrow all members came and went as they chose, their minds in contact with the others. Once again he regretted the mischief Rowan was risking. He felt her nervousness about that, and was not able to make it much easier for her to bear, because the risk was real.

Outside, she put Peba on the ground. "Lead and I'll follow," she thought. "Remember, I'll get tangled if we go through brambles, and I'll fall if there are holes. I can hardly see anything out here."

Peba scurried along, sniffing out a suitable path for the girl to follow. Then he sent her his awareness of the ground, its sight, smell, and feel, and that enabled her to place her feet with much greater certainty. They moved well.

"I feel like an armadillo," she thought. "This is fun!"

In due course the reached the sinkhole. They moved down into it, and entered the cave. "They are here," Peba thought. "They know the way."

"We are here," Gopher agreed.

"Good, because we'll have to hurry. Mr. Klondike won't wait for us."

She put Cottontail in one bag, and Gopher in the other. "Who else needs a ride?"

No one else did. Peba and Indigo walked and slithered, and Owl flew, all knowing the direction from the girl's mind. They hurried toward the neighbor's house.

They were in time. Rowan lifted Peba and Indigo into the back of the truck, and set the open bags there too. Owl came down to join them. Rowan covered them all over with what she called a tarpaulin, and they waited.

Soon the neighbor come out. He did not check the back of the truck; he just got into the front. "The motor will start," Rowan thought. "Don't spook."

There was a roar, and the whole truck shook. They all would have spooked, but for Rowan's reassuring thoughts. As it was, they were nervous enough. "This is like my captivity," Gopher thought. "I do not like it."

"This is a different truck," Rowan assured him. "Mr. Klondike doesn't hunt tortoises."

Then the truck moved. It lurched forward. They all hated it, but again the girl reassured them.

The truck continued to shake. "It's rolling along the road," Rowan explained. "That's how folk travel here. It's uncomfortable, but very fast."

They bore with it. In fact Peba was able to reach out and sense the mind of the neighbor, Mr. Klondike, and feel his rapport with the vehicle as he guided it. He shared that awareness with the others, and that helped.

After some time, the truck gave a final lurch, stopped, and the vibrating motor stopped. The man left the truck; they felt his mind depart.

"This is Tangletree. Now comes the tricky part," Rowan thought. "We have to catch a truck going south. I'll have to carry all of you, and you will have to check the nearby minds to see which is best."

Peba shared a bag with Owl and Cottontail, while Gopher and Indigo were in the other. Rowan carried them in her two hands, walking between parked cars and trucks. Their combined weight tired her arms, so they lent her strength and she managed. She walked close outside what she termed a restaurant, a place where humans gathered to eat. Cottontail reassured them about its nature, having had experience with one. There were several humans there.

They reached out to feel the nearest minds. "Find one who is going south to Horseman's Estate," Rowan thought. "There is bound to be one."

They searched, touching one mind after another. Then they found one. "That's our man," Rowan thought. "Find out which truck is his."

In the man's mind was an image of a dull green truck with a load of horsefeed. "That has to be it," Rowan thought. "Now we must find it and get aboard."

They walked through the parking lot. There were a number of cars, but not many trucks, so it was easy to find. "Say, this is one of those trucks with a sleeping chamber," Rowan thought. "So the driver can pull over and sleep when he's tired, without having to look for a motel to stay in. He's close to where he's going; he probably won't check it. He'll just get in and drive."

"Suppose he does check?" Peba asked. He had not enjoyed the ride in the other truck, and did not trust this new one. None of this was like tunneling through the ground.

"I'll have to go into my lost little girl act, and you'll have to touch his mind to make him believe me. But I hope we can avoid that."

But Indigo slithered to another aspect. "We have not had much experience touching human minds other than Rowan's. Only Cottontail has done it. We need practice, so as to be ready for this Dayson Human Man. We should try this Truck Human Man."

There was general agreement. "Oh, my, you're right," Rowan thought. "It freaks me out, but we should tackle him up front. Then if it goes wrong, we'll know better when we get to Dayson."

"Prepare your Innocent Girl act," Cottontail thought. "We will enhance it as we orient on the man's mind."

"You'd better, because what I'm doing out here at night is enough to get me canned if the folks catch on." Rowan had tied back her hair; now she loosened it and shook it out so that it fell across her shoulders. Peba knew from her mind that this made her look more like a Girl.

"He is coming," Owl thought. He had been keeping a

lookout, doing a mental overview.

Rowan stood beside the truck. Peba felt her heart beating rapidly; she was quite nervous about this. "We must calm her," he thought. "We must give her assurance."

They worked on it, and the girl did gain confidence. "That's some trick," she thought. "You boys are better than a pill."

The man paused as he spied Rowan. "What are you doing out here at night, kid?" he demanded.

"I got stranded, and I've just *got* to get home to Horseman's estate," Rowan said. "Please, mister, will you let me ride with you?"

"I'm not supposed to pick up passengers," he said. "Particularly not children."

"Please," Rowan repeated tearfully.

Peba and the others were addressing the man's mind. It was closed, but Cottontail had found out how to find crevices, and they were able to get in. They concentrated on Belief, Acceptance, and Sympathy.

"Aw, okay," the man said. "I shouldn't, but what the hell. I mean heck." They felt his embarrassment; it seemed that there were some vocal words that weren't supposed to be used on children, so he substituted another word that meant the same thing. This was tricky for Peba to understand, but was a good sign. The man would help. "I'm going there anyway."

"Thank you so much," Rowan said, smiling bravely.

"Get in the cab. Here; I'll toss your bags in back."

"No!" Rowan cried. "Things would break." She walked around to the other door, carrying the bags herself. She opened the door and lifted the two bags in very carefully. Peba appreciated that; he did not much like being bagged, and being bounced around was worse.

The man made the truck motor start, and they moved out onto the road. Peba and the others were able to see some through the man's eyes. They were getting better at this; it was like directing a human mind in their own realm, once they made allowances for its closed nature and its awesome power.

"So who are you?" the man inquired. "How did you

get stranded?"

Rowan talked, and none of what she said was true. This was another new concept: lying. It seemed that the humans of this realm did it a lot. They were able to, because their minds were closed; they could not read each other's thoughts.

Meanwhile the members of the burrow were getting good practice, discovering the aspects of this mind that led to belief and acceptance. There were large areas it was better to avoid, such as the complications of the hauling business, bad drivers, and family life, so they focused on the more familiar ones, such as where he was going and what he looked forward to eating next. If the Dayson mind was similar to this one, they would know how to influence it.

"Do you know where Dayson Consultancies is?" Rowan inquired.

"That's where you're going? Sure, I've seen the sign. But it's out of my way."

"Go there anyway," Peba thought firmly, buttressed by the other minds.

"But it won't hurt to vary my route a little."

He took them to the address, and Rowan got out with her bags, thanking him. "But better make him forget all this, if you can," she thought.

They concentrated as the man drove away, making him forget. That was another useful exercise. They were getting better at the manipulation of closed powerful human minds; they answered to the same commands as the dull humans back home, when the directives were strong enough and correctly phrased. But it would not have been possible for a single burrow mate to do it, or even two or three; it took all of them to mount enough mental power to do it effectively. Cottontail had been right about that.

Now they were at the house of the key man. Rowan walked around to the back of the house where it was dark, and opened the bags so the burrow mates could come out. That was a relief. They walked around the small yard, and Owl flew up to perch on a fence. Then he spread out his awareness.

"The human man is sleeping," Owl reported.

"Do we have to wake him?" Rowan asked.

"No. We can implant thoughts in a sleeping human mind more readily than in a waking one, because they turn off their conscious choices. In fact, this one seems considerably more open, being in a dreaming state."

"Good. Can you do it from here?"

Owl considered. "No. We need to get close, and focus intensely, or the command will not remain after we depart. Normally we direct humans only for the moment, and are not concerned with what they think at other times. We want this change to be permanent."

"I don't think we can get inside very readily," Rowan thought. "The house is bound to have an alarm system." She sent them a new concept of a machine that lurked like a cat, eager to pounce if anyone came in range. It would make a loud noise and call in the police, who were like predators. That daunted them.

"If one of us gets close to the human man, the others can work through that one," Gopher thought. "Who can get inside without disturbing the alarm?

"I can tunnel there," Peba thought. "Would that do?"

"I think it would," Rowan agreed. "The alarm wires probably cover the doors and windows, but not the ground. But the house should be on a concrete base."

Peba sniffed around the house. "There is a place where there is dirt below the wall."

"Well, maybe this is an older house, and part of it projects beyond the concrete," Rowan thought. "If you can get in there, maybe you can locate him once you're inside the house."

"I will try," Peba agreed. He started digging by the wall, using his strong front claws, and soon excavated a hole under the wall. Gopher could tunnel, but Peba was faster, and his armored body was more flexible than Gopher's shell. He angled up on the other side. Soon he was inside the house.

At least he was inside something. It was dark, and his feet and nose told him more than his eyes did. "There is not a large space here," he reported.

"What size is it?" thought came.

Peba sniffed and felt, describing the size.

"That's a crawlway," Rowan thought. "A sort of space under the house where there are pipes and things You should be able to find a way out of it and into the house proper. I think."

Peba ran along the low passage, which was somewhat like a tunnel. He came to something hot.

"That's a hot water pipe," Rowan thought. "Avoid it."

Finally he found an aperture to another chamber. "I think that's where pipes or something used to be," Rowan thought. "See if it leads into the main house."

It seemed to, but there was a closed door blocking the way. "Maybe it's not closed all the way," Rowan thought. "Try pushing against it, slowly."

Peba put his back against it and pushed. The door moved. Soon there was a big enough opening for him to pass through. Now he was in the main house.

"Woof!"

That was a dog, making a vocal sound along with its thought. Peba curled up into a ball. The dog sniffed at him, trying to figure him out.

"A dog!" Rowan thought. "I never thought of that. Can we stop it?"

"We can send it a sleep signal," Indigo thought. "We will send it through you, Peba."

The signal came, amplified by the joined minds of the burrow mates. Peba oriented on the dog, finding its mind, and sent the sleep signal there. Then the dog lay down and slept.

Peba uncurled and went on. "Where is the human man?" he asked.

"That way," Owl replied, sending a direction.

Peba followed it, and come to another door. He was able to wedge it open and enter what Rowan thought was the bedroom. The human man was sleeping on the bed.

"Get close to him," Gopher thought. "Then relay the signal."

Peba went under the bed, orienting on the sleeping mind. When he was directly beneath it, he lifted his nose as high as he could. He searched for the entry into the mind, getting his thought placed there.

"That's it," Cottontail thought. "Now we will channel our thought through you."

Peba held his position while the massed thought built up. "CHANGE THE MALL LOCATION. THE SINKHOLE IS NOT GOOD. PUT IT AT THE OTHER SITE."

The human man stirred in his sleep, disturbed by the mental intrusion. But the thought had been implanted. He would wake and think it was his own. If this worked.

"Now get out of there," Rowan thought. "Hurry!"

Peba scurried from under the bed, out the doorway, past the sleeping dog, through the other door, through the old pipe hole, and into the crawlway. Now that the mental contact was broken, both the man and dog woke. The dog started barking, and the man got off his bed; Peba felt their changing mind traces. He hurried.

Soon he reached his tunnel under the wall, and wedged through it. "We'd better fill this in," Rowan thought. She scraped at the dirt with her hands. "We don't want them to know what happened."

Gopher and Peba helped scrape dirt into the hole, and Rowan tamped it tight with her feet. Then they got into the two bags and the girl carried them around and away from the house. They were escaping!

But now they had a problem: getting back. There was no truck with a cooperative driver; in fact very few cars were on the road at this hour.

Peba realized that they had been so focused on reaching the key man, and changing his mind, that they hadn't thought about what happened afterward. They had accomplished their mission; the Dayson man would surely have the Mall site changed. But what good would that be if all of them were stuck well away from the portal?

"Suddenly I'm not feeling very smart," Rowan thought glumly. "I may have gotten all of us into deep manure." The last image was of a big pit filled with ill-smelling refuse, a loathsome place to be. It seemed that this was another concept with different vocal words, some of which were not supposed to be spoken or heard by children. Rowan had used a bad word. She was clearly an unreformed child.

None of the burrow mates wanted to be in that particular pit, whatever its word. "What alternatives are there?" Peba asked.

"Just one, I think," Rowan thought. "I think I'll have to hitchhike."

There were dark thoughts associated with this concept. "Is there danger?" Peba asked for them all.

"Yes. You never can tell who will pick you up. But we'll have to do it, and I hope you folk can change the mind of any bad man. It's the only way."

"We will try," Peba agreed.

Rowan walked to what she thought of as a through street, with cars traveling along it, then stood beside the pavement and stuck out her thumb. The first car passed on by, and the next, but then one slowed and stopped. It had colored lights lights on it; Peba saw them through the girl's mind.

"Oh, no!" she thought. "A police car!"

Her mind made it clear: this was disaster. The police were humans who enforced the rules of the human society. Children were not supposed to be out on the road at night, especially not hitchhiking. Rowan could not escape them, and the burrow mates could not change the police minds in time to do any good. Rowan was captive, and the burrow mates with her.

This was truly deep manure.

Chapter 7
Prisoner

Owl was as nervous as the other burrow mates. The Police had captured them, and only desperate avoidance broadcasting had stopped the humans from taking and opening Rowan's bags and discovering the animals. But that merely postponed the danger; all of them remained captive, and it was not clear how they would escape.

The Police car arrived at Rowan's house. Uncle and Aunt came out to meet them; they would have been called, Rowan's mind thought. These inordinately smart humans had ways of contacting each other at a distance that rivaled telepathy. The car stopped, the policemen got out, and one of them came around to open the door nearest to Rowan. She scrambled out, hauling the bags with her.

Aunt turned to face her, from the other side of the car. "Go to your room," her terse thought came. "We will attend to you in a moment."

Rowan walked to the house. Her mind said that it was best not to show any resistance at this time, lest the situation worsen yet more. Then, when Uncle and Aunt were talking with the Policemen, she paused by a bush before the door. She set down the two bags so that the bush concealed them from the other humans, and opened them. "Go!" she thought urgently. "Get out of here. Go through the portal and don't come back. They'll never know you were here, and you'll be safe." But behind her thought there was sheer misery, for she believed she would never see them again.

"I can't do that," Cottontail thought.

"Oh that's right, you can't walk. I'm so sorry. I'll have to keep you with me. I'll tell them I found you injured, and they won't know your nature." She reached into the bag to lift Cottontail out.

Meanwhile the other animals got out of sight under the bushes. Peba, Indigo, and Owl were gone immediately; Gopher was of course slower, but had no trouble finding concealment. Owl found a perch under a thick shrub and remained put, so he could focus on the minds of the others.

Rowan picked up the empty bags, letting Cottontail cling to her shoulder. She went into the house.

Now the five burrow mates held a conference. "We will not leave you here," Gopher thought to Cottontail, for all of them. "We will rescue you."

"You must rescue Rowan also," Cottontail thought. "So she can carry me to the portal."

"We will try."

But Owl knew that he was not the only one who feared that was not possible. These smart humans were dangerous.

Soon the group by the Police car ended its discussion, and Uncle and Aunt returned to the house. They locked Rowan in her room, not even inquiring how she was. They were angry; that emotion came through their closed minds. The Police car drove away, but the anger remained. This boded no good for Rowan.

Gopher remained close to the house, circling it so as to get close to Rowan's room. The other burrow mates went the other way, getting closer to the adult humans. They focused on their minds, trying to get inside so as to influence them.

"They are going to send Rowan away," Indigo reported. "To something called a boarding school. They don't want her here any more."

Owl was alarmed. "But our whole effort here is to keep the portal open so we can remain in touch."

Cottontail's thought came from inside the house. "I am informing Rowan of their plan for her. She is extremely upset."

Indeed, Owl felt the girl's misery. "Inform her that we will rescue her, just as she rescued Gopher." Though he had no idea how.

Now Rowan's thought came, as she focused. "Owl! You have to get away from here. Don't let them catch you!"

"We are learning to make them forget us," Owl reminded her. "And we must not let Cottontail be lost."

"Oh, you're right! I forgot about him, though I'm holding him. But how can he get back to the portal?"

"We will free you, and you will carry him," Owl thought. "But you must show us how to free you." maybe her larger mind could find an answer.

"You're all here? You didn't go to the portal? Yes, now I feel your minds. But the danger! If you get caught—if something goes wrong—"

"You are getting more flighty than I am," Owl reproved her. "How can we free you?"

"Gee, fellas, I'm crying!" And she was, but they understood from her mind that this was in this case a positive expression of emotion. She appreciated their support. "But I'll try to figure something out. What we need is the key." There was a mental picture of a small metal object that was used to lock and unlock a door. "But that will be in Aunt's purse. No way to get that. Unless one of you can sneak inside and fetch it. And you can't do that, because the outer doors are locked too. They're not taking any chances tonight."

"Peba can tunnel under."

"Not this house; it's on a solid concrete slab And the windows are all closed, and if any broke, they'd be alert right away. You'd have to come down the chimney." She paused, a wild idea coming. "The chimney! They're not using the fireplace in the summer. If someone could come down that, it just might work."

Owl did not ponder long. "I will do it."

Now Rowan protested. "But it's dangerous! You could get stuck in there, or suffocate. You couldn't fly in there, and you'd get so awfully dirty you'd hate it."

"I am a burrowing owl," he reminded her. "I am accustomed to tight dirty tunnels. I can preen after the job is done." all this was true, but he remained nervous about the task. He had on occasion experienced the ashes of burned-over sections of the forest, and did not relish being confined in that sort of thing.

"You're so brave," Rowan thought.

"It is merely a job to do." But he was pleased by her flattery. That powerful mind had strong feelings too, and when the girl was pleased, *he* was pleased. He did like her; they all did. So he had to do his part to save her. "I will fly up to the chimney opening."

"We will support you in whatever way we can," Gopher thought. "But we can do nothing physically."

"I will manage." Owl moved out from the bush, then launched into the air. He felw to the top of the house, where the chimney poked up. He perched on its brick rim. He sent out a picture of what he saw.

"That's it," Rowan thought. "Oh—I don't know if there's a damper!"

"What is that?"

"It's a sort of metal thing that shuts off the air. I think most chimneys have them. I really don't know much about chimneys. Maybe you better not do this."

But Owl was already jumping into the chimney, lest he get too nervous to continue. There was soot, but there was also room to spread his wings somewhat. He could handle this.

He dropped down, using his half-spread wings to slow his fall. This scraped soot off the sides, but that couldn't be helped. When it got too dark to see well, he spread his wings farther and slowed almost to a stop. That was just as well, because he was coming to the bottom. No, it was an angled piece of metal.

"That's the damper," Rowan thought. "I guess you could push it farther open if you need to."

"I don't need to," he replied, sliding past it. One advantage of being a small owl was that he could get into places other owls could not manage. That made it easier to join the burrow; most birds were limited to tree branches. Living underground also protected him from extremes of weather; he didn't have to get wet or cold or hot, because things were pretty stable down in the burrow. The gopher tortoises had made a good thing when they went below. But most of all, his burrow experience enabled him to handle something like this chimney, now that he needed to.

"You're wonderful, Owl," Rowan agreed.

He hadn't been trying to broadcast that, but she had picked it up anyway. She was improving.

"It's because we're in continuing contact," she thought. "I couldn't read your thoughts if you weren't letting me. Just as I couldn't see anything in this darkness if you weren't letting me use your eyes."

True. But she was still improving. And he liked her.

"I like you too, Owl. I like all of you in the burrow. That's why I want to stay in touch. But so far I've mostly gotten us all in trouble."

"We all got us all in trouble," he thought. "We held a burrow meeting and decided. We want to remain in touch with you too."

He had been working his way down; now he was at the bottom. It was an arched niche, with a metal grate for his feet to grasp, and ashes below it.

"You're in the fireplace," Rowan thought. "Shake yourself off there, because you don't want to track soot all through the house and leave evidence of what you're doing."

Owl hadn't thought of that. In the forest or burrow such refuse hardly mattered; it just fell to the ground and was trampled down. But now he understood how black soot could make a trail that a human could follow, and that would be bad if it happened before he escaped the house. So he shook himself, beat his wings in place while holding on to the grate, and did a fast crude preening. He got much of the soot off, but it would take time to do the whole job.

"Mainly your feet, and what will shed when you fly," Rowan suggested. "It won't hurt if you leave a little."

Then a dark shape loomed. Owl froze, but the thing had already spotted him during his distraction with the soot shedding. It was a cat!

"Oh my goodness!" Rowan thought. "I forgot about the cat! That's Frag!"

"A cat!" That was Cottontail's horror.

Then it all poured in from her mind: Uncle and Aunt had a fat orange tabby cat named Dleifrag. Rowan didn't like him, as he was a fat lazy creature whose main entertainment was squashing innocent spiders and trying to catch birds. So she had ignored him. He was easy to ignore, as he slept most of the time he wasn't eating, and wasn't very social. But now he could not be ignored.

In fact, seeing Owl aware of him, Frag pounced. Owl flapped his wings and shot up the chimney, just out of reach. The cat snarled and swept at the bricks, trying to catch Owl. He couldn't—but neither could Owl get by him to complete his mission. This was a real problem.

"Darn it!" Rowan thought. "I'd never have let you go there if I'd remembered Frag. You'd better just scoot up the chimney and save your tail."

Now Peba's thought came. "No. We put the dog to sleep. We can put the cat to sleep."

"Say, that's right!" Rowan thought. "If we can make him sleep, then it'll be halfway safe. Maybe. But he's an ornery beast, and he's never short of sleep. So I don't know."

"We will focus," Gopher thought. It was his job as burrow master to speak for all of them, and to organize things. "all except Owl and Rowan, because they need to concentrate on their mission."

Owl felt the others focusing on the cat. Frag felt it too; he turned and spat at nothing, trying to find an enemy he sensed but could not see or smell. The harder they concentrated, the more the ornery cat fought. He was definitely not going to sleep.

Then Rowan had an idea. "We don't need Frag to be asleep, we just need him to be somewhere else. Maybe we can distract him, so Owl can get through."

"I'll do it," Cottontail thought. "Mentally is much better than physically."

Owl felt the rabbit concentrate. The others supported him, adding to his thought. A picture of him formed before the cat. At first it was fuzzy in outline, then it firmed. But the cat did not pay attention to it.

"It's in image, not a real rabbit," Rowan thought. "Like a picture. It needs to smell and sound like a rabbit too."

"Give me your mind," Indigo thought. "I will make it smell like you." In a moment the odor of warm rabbit wafted bout from the image. Indigo knew the smell of rabbits, because he hunted them on occasion.

"And I will make it sound like you," Gopher thought. The beat of feet on the ground came.

"And I will make it move like you," Peba thought. The figure lifted its ears, turned about, and looked at the cat.

Suddenly Frag believed. He turned and pounced on the image, but it zipped out of the way. An armadillo could move quite quickly when it wanted to. There was the sound of feet striking the floor; they did not quite match the image's landing, but it took a while for the four minds to coordinate perfectly.

Frag whirled and pounced again. He was quite agile for a fat cat. But the image rabbit was already scooting for another room in the house, trailing its smell.

The cat ran after it, and this time caught it. And the image passed right through Frag's paws and moved on.

"Now if that were me, I'd catch on that it's a ghost," Rowan thought. "But I don't think Frag's that smart."

It did set the cat back, though. He paused, not pursuing for a moment. Then the rabbit faced back and wiggled its ears teasingly. The armadillo's little ears could move like that, so it was realistic.

Furious, the cat pounced again—and missed. The rabbit ran out of the room. The cat followed.

"Now we can get by," Roman thought. "But it's still dangerous. If Frag gives up on the ghost—"

"I'll poop in his face," Cottontail thought. "I'll bite his tail. This is fun!"

"I guess if you can keep him mad, he won't pause to think," Rowan thought. "But Owl, you'd better get done as fast as you can, just in case. And I'll prepare a stun thought, also just in case."

Owl dropped down again, shook himself out, then followed the girl's guidance to the humans' bedroom. He heard the cat moving in another room, and that made him nervous. But if the cat appeared, he would spread his wings and fly as rapidly as possible to the fireplace, and up the chimney. He wasn't sure a stun thought would stop this creature, but it might slow it down enough.

"Okay, now we have to find Aunt's purse," Rowan thought. "It should be near her side of the bed."

Owl hopped along the floor toward the bed. He felt the mental nearness of Aunt as she slept, and heard her faint breathing. He didn't like being this close to her, but of course it couldn't be avoided.

"There it is," Rowan thought. "Up on that bed table."

Owl looked up. He saw the shape she meant. But he was on the floor, and it was up there. He would have to fly up.

"Can you do it quietly?"

"I am an owl," he reminded her. He spread his wings and flew silently up, landing on the table beside the purse.

But the purse was closed. "You will have to work the zipper," Rowan thought. "Like this." She made a mental image of catching hold of a little tag and pulling it back along the fastening.

Owl caught the tag in his beak and pulled. It resisted.

"Change the angle."

He did so—and suddenly the tag yielded. Caught off-balance, he scrambled across the table, still holding the tag. Then he fell off the edge of the table. He jerked on the tag, trying to recover, but instead pulled the purse over the edge with him. He spread his wings as he let go, getting clear of it. It fell to the floor with a solid thunk, and some of its contents spilled out.

"Oopsy!" Rowan thought.

The sleeping figure woke. Aunt sat up. "What was that?" her sharp thought came.

"Grab the key and run!" Rowan thought. "I mean fly!" Her thought showed exactly where and what the key was.

Owl pounced on the key, getting it in his beak.

Aunt did something. Suddenly there was blinding light. Owl, dazed, could not move.

Aunt saw him. "Eeeee!!" she screamed.

"Get out of here!" Rowan thought urgently. "This way!" She made a mental map of the room, showing the way out.

Still blinded, Owl followed her direction. In a moment he was in the darker part of the house and could see again.

And almost banged into Frag, who was charging toward the commotion in the bedroom. Owl leaped, spreading his wings, and the cat passed right under him.

"Fly to the chimney!" Rowan thought. "While they're distracted. Get out of the house!"

"But you need the key," Indigo's thought reminded them.

"It's too dangerous!" Rowan thought. "They're all up and active. Owl has to get out immediately."

"After I do the job," Owl thought. He flew to Rowan's bedroom with the key.

"You're so brave!" she thought again. "But I'll never forgive myself if—"

But now the door blocked him. He could not use the key himself. "What can I do?"

"Put it down by the crack under the door. Push it under as far as you can, so I can fetch it from this side. Then I'll be able to use it."

Owl dropped the key on the floor and nudged it into the crevice. Then it disappeared. "I got it!" Rowan thought. "Thank you so much, Owl! Now get to that chimney!"

Owl turned—and there was Frag barring his way. The cat had gotten straightened out enough to get back on the trail. This time Frag had no intention of being led astray by a ghost rabbit. His eyes were fixed on Owl and his muscles were tensing.

"The bomb!" Rowan thought. "Send it right to the cat! Here it comes!"

Owl braced as her violent thought surged into his mind. It was sheer rage, focused on the cat. He channeled it to the largest crevice in the animal's closed mind. **POW!**

Frag rocked back, half stunned. He was dazed but not out, and when owl started to move, the feline eyes still tracked him. He knew that cats pounced largely on instinct, so it wasn't safe to try to pass close by. But neither was it safe to remain here. Soon the cat's head would clear, and then he would pounce anyway.

"Maybe make multiple owls," Rowan thought. "Each run by a different burrow mate. Can you do that?"

"We can do it," Tortoise thought. "If Owl gives us his mind."

"Take it," Owl thought. "Otherwise I'm dead."

Tortoise entered his mind, made himself into an image, and moved away. A ghost Owl moved with him. Then Peba entered, and made another image. Then Indigo, and Cottontail. Four ghost Owls were in the room.

Frag looked dazedly from one to the other. Then he pounced on the nearest—and passed right through it.

Another Owl moved before the cat's face. "Hoooot!" he thought. It hardly sounded like a real burrowing owl, but it fooled the cat, who pounced on it—and found nothing.

Then all four Owls were surrounding the cat, teasing him, picking at his tail, hooting, and fluffing feathers in his face. Frag swiped at them, getting nowhere.

Meanwhile the real Owl moved quietly around and out the door. Then he flew to the fireplace. In a moment he was scrambling up the chimney, heedless of the soot. At last he reached the top. He sat on the roof of the house and shook out his feathers. He was safe—and he had accomplished his mission.

"I am out," he thought to the others. "You can let the ghosts go."

"Gone," Tortoise agreed. "That was fun."

"And I've got the key," Rowan agreed. "But I can't use it yet, because Uncle and Aunt are still up."

"Aunt is coming to your room," Cottontail thought urgently. "To see if you are all right."

"Oh, no! If she wants to come in, she'll have to use the key, and then she'll realize it's gone. I'll try to bluff her.

Can you make her believe?"

"We will focus on her," Tortoise thought.

Owl joined in, seeking access to the woman's mind. Each new closed mind was a challenge, but they all had crevices so that it was possible to get inside a little. Cottontail had found the best crevice, so the others were using that.

Aunt came and knocked on Rowan's door. Her thought came through clearly, because it was vocalized and Rowan's mind translated it. "Dear, are you all right? Something very strange is happening."

"Is something wrong?" Rowan thought to Aunt, vocalizing similarly. "I was asleep. I'm all right."

Owl and the others made a concerted push of acceptance. There was no need to open the door; Rowan was all right.

The woman hesitated a moment, then was swayed by the will to believe. "Very well, dear; go back to sleep."

"Sure will, Aunt," Rowan replied.

Aunt returned to her room, where Uncle awaited her. "I saw an owl in the house! And something was arousing Dleifrag; he was rushing all over."

"An owl!" Uncle thought. "What would it be doing in the house?"

"I have no idea. I see no sign of it now."

"Must have been a bad dream. Get back to bed; we need our sleep. Got a big day tomorrow."

"Yes. Of course we'll have to tell Rowan where she's going. We just can't handle a child who willfully disobeys rules."

"They'll take good care of her at the summer boarding school. She might even like it."

"She's simply too wild for us. That must be why her family sent her away."

Then they turned off the lights and settled down. Soon, encouraged by the burrow mates' massed sleep signals, they slept.

"Good," Rowan thought. "Try to keep them that way. I'm writing them a note."

"What is a note?" Owl asked from the roof.

"Just a little bit of thought put on a paper," Rowan explained, sending the new concept out. "I'm telling them not to worry, because I'm fine. I'm just going somewhere else."

She finished the note and left it on the little table by the bed. She had already packed her things; Cottontail had to share a bag with some of her clothing. Fortunately it was soft.

Then Rowan used the key to unlock the bedroom door. As she opened the door and stepped through, cautiously in the darkness, she had another thought: "Maybe I should lock it again, so they don't know how I got out. And I'll return the key to Aunt's purse. It'll be a real locked-room mystery."

The burrow mates focused, keeping Aunt and uncle asleep as Rowan quietly entered their bedroom and returned the key to Aunt's purse. Then the girl moved to the front door of the house and tried to open it. It didn't budge.

"Oopsy! It's locked, of course! I need the key—but then I won't be able to return it to Aunt's purse, and the mystery will be ruined." She stood a moment in indecision.

"Can you go up the chimney?" Owl thought.

Rowan made a mental laugh. "I'm way too big and clumsy for that! No, I'll go out a window. Only the bedroom one is boarded up." She went to a window, opened it, set her two bags outside, climbed out, and closed it carefully after her.

Indigo and Peba joined her, and Gopher made his way toward her more slowly. Owl flew down.

"Well, I guess we're on our way," Rowan thought. "We'll get you folk to the portal, and I'll set Cottontail in the tunnel and hope he can make it the rest of the way. Then—"

Owl understood the pause. Rowan had not thought beyond the point of rescuing Cottontail. What was she to do, once the burrow mates were safely on their way?

Chapter 8
Transformation

Tortoise had the answer: "You will come with us."

"To your realm? Oh, I'd love that! But I'd never fit through that tunnel."

"We will widen it."

They all felt the dawning hope in her mind. "You can do that? You can let me in?"

"Peba and I are good tunnelers," Tortoise thought. "It may take time, but we can do it. You have no house to stay in now, so you must find residence in our realm. We can remain together."

"Oh, that's so wonderful! I'm crying again. I always wanted to see your world, I mean your realm, but never thought I would."

They moved on toward the sink hole. Rowan picked up Gopher and made a place for him in her other bag, so that they could move faster. Then she thought of another thing. "Maybe we shouldn't go directly there, because we'll leave footprints and things, and they'll trace us and find the portal. We'd better take a roundabout route."

That made sense, as they assimilated the concept in her mind. So though they were all tired from the long night's adventures, they took the long route. It was near dawn by the time they entered the sinkhole from the far side. They entered the cave and came to the tunnel to their own realm.

Now Gopher and Peba got to work. They started at the top of the ramp and dug at either side of the tunnel, rapidly sending the dirt down into the cave. Peba was the faster digger, but Gopher was steadier. Meanwhile Owl and Indigo helped move the dirt to the sides of the ramp, and Rowan used her hands to push masses of it aside. "Wish I had a shovel," she thought.

"You are tired," Gopher thought. "You must rest, for the digging will take time."

"We're all tired," Rowan thought. "We all need rest, after being active all night. But if we delay, and they find us before we get through—"

"Perhaps we should block the cave, so others do not come here," Indigo suggested.

"But then we couldn't stay in contact!" Rowan protested.

"You are on this side." And he had slithered to an insight others had missed: Rowan was with them, and they would need no more to rendezvous. It was more important to block the cave so that stray humans would not find the portal, and reopen it themselves when they had reason.

"You're right," she thought, pleased. "I wasn't thinking straight."

"Because you are tired," Gopher reminded her. "Rest, and you may help dig when we tire."

"Got it." Rowan made herself a bed in soft dirt and lay down. Cottontail kept her company. After a moment, Owl and Indigo joined them.

Gopher and Peba continued to dig, sending huge masses of dirt down into the cave. When it started clogging the tunnel behind them they had to stop. At that point Rowan and the others woke, and worked to move it toward the cave entrance while the two diggers rested.

They continued alternating shifts for some time. They were getting hungry, but the work had to continue. They checked the size of the enlarged tunnel, and found that Rowan could fit if she wriggled; she was not as big as she seemed, when she moved snakelike along it.

But as they worked, Indigo came up with a problem:

"She is alien to our realm, and far too intelligent for her kind. Her nature must be concealed."

As usual, the snake had slithered into an aspect the others had missed. It was true: Rowan Girl was not at all like the dull humans of the home realm, and would not fit in among them. In fact she would need to be protected from them, for they could be cruel to any of their kind that were different in any way. How could they handle this?

He asked Rowan, who was not far behind him as she used her hands to scoop away the dirt he dug. "You will not like our humans," he thought to her. "But you will not fit in our burrow. How can we keep you safe?"

"Maybe I can stay somewhere else," she replied. "Somewhere nearby, and you can keep in mental touch with me. Is there any suitable place?"

"There is one," Cottontail thought. "The bear cave."

"Bears!" Rowan thought, alarmed. "I'm afraid of bears."

"We are all cautious of bears," Gopher thought. "But these are well behaved, or they would not be tolerated in our area. They hunt only in approved regions, and do not bother burrow mates."

"Oh, like trained bears. I guess that would be all right, if you're sure they won't hurt me."

"We shall have to make a deal," Indigo thought. "Those bears are hungry."

"Hungry!" Rowan thought, alarmed again.

"That means they will deal for food," Gopher clarified. "Where is there food for them?"

"I know that," Owl thought. "There is a rogue band of pigs foraging not far from our burrow. I have seen them in my flights. Someone will have to deal with them before long, and perhaps we should be the ones."

"We could nudge them toward the bear cave," Indigo thought. "In return for a favor."

"Safe refuge for the human girl," Gopher agreed, seeing it. "We must arrange it. Peba and I must continue digging; who can see to the pigs and bears?"

"I can nudge the pigs," Owl thought. "I will hide near them and send thoughts of good foraging near the bears' cave."

"I can negotiate with the bears," Indigo thought. "I am a hunter, and understand their nature. But their minds are dull; I will need more mental power than my own to forge the deal clearly."

"I could help," Cottontail thought. "But I am afraid of bears, and can't move fast enough." A tweak of pain reminded them of his hurt foot.

"Can I help?" Rowan asked. "Maybe if Cottontail hooks on to my mind and projects it to Indigo."

"That should work," Indigo agreed. "You can help Owl also, so that he can have greater impact on the pigs." He slithered rapidly ahead, and Owl followed.

Gopher kept digging. He was tired, but felt better; they were acting as burrow mates should, solving a problem together. Actually they were approaching the burrow proper; there was a gully near it where this off-tunnel exited, and they would take the girl there.

Owl emerged and took wing; his thoughts came back to Gopher. It was getting near dawn, and the pigs were stirring; they preferred to forage at dawn and dusk, when it wasn't as hot or cold as full day or night. Gopher saw them through Owl's eyes: a big brutish boar with twisted tusks, and several younger sows who followed his lead. He remembered that they had torn up the soil near an established burrow, and been warned off. They had moved on grudgingly, and were paying less attention to the concerns of sapient animals. They had ignored warnings to leave this region. Owl was correct: they were a rogue band, and soon would have to be dealt with, because ornery pigs were dangerous.

"I don't understand," Rowan thought. "Why can't they forage in the forest?"

"They are too efficient," Cottontail explained. "A tortoise will eat only certain types of leaves and grass, as will a rabbit. A snake eats a mouse or other animal only once in several days. All of us are fairly choosy eaters, so we don't do much harm. But pigs eat anything, and when they pass through, there is nothing left for anyone else. Other creatures go hungry and have to move away—and that makes them intrude on the territories of others. So it gets complicated. We can't afford to have rogue pigs in our area."

"Oh, I see. So you ask them to go elsewhere."

"Yes, and if they do, we leave them alone. But a rogue band stops listening, and then there is trouble."

Owl perched on a branch just above the stirring pigs. "Lend me some mind," he thought.

"May I borrow yours?" Cottontail asked.

"Sure."

Gopher, still digging, felt the rabbit merge with the girl's huge mind. Then they connected with Owl, who shaped the thought into a directive to the boar. "Good forage this way."

The boar snorted and started in that direction, and the sows followed. They were on the way.

Meanwhile Indigo reached the bear cave. "Dialogue," he thought to the most open minded bear, which was a young male.

"What you want, snake?" the bear demanded gruffly in its limited mind talk. Bears were only half sapient.

"I am with the nearby burrow," Indigo replied. "We want to make a deal."

"Come closer, snake, and I eat you," the bear thought.

"We offer much richer food. But we want something from you in return."

The bear mulled this over. "What you want?"

"Sanctuary for a human girl. Safe rest, protection." then, to clarify it: "No hurt girl."

The bear found this funny, and so did his companions. "No hurt girl! What you offer, better than tasty girl?"

"Pigs. Here."

Suddenly Indigo had their whole attention. "Pigs we can catch?"

"Pigs you can eat. We will bring them here. You let girl sleep."

"We fill bellies, we let girl be. Deal."

"Deal. Pigs come soon. Girl come later. Remember."

"Deal," the bear agreed.

"I will stay with the girl, to remind you."

"Deal."

"Go outside. Pigs come soon."

The bears filed out. In a moment they disappeared into the brush near the cave entrance. Indigo relayed the picture.

Meanwhile Owl was guiding the pigs toward the cave. The bears, impatient to get on with the hunt, moved quietly through the brush to intercept them.

Gopher returned his attention to Rowan. "We must hide you until we can properly care for you. I feel how tired you are. We are all tired, and must rest for a day. You will be safe with the bears, until we can make it right."

"Make it right?"

"There are protocols. We must establish you as a regular subject human. Then no one will suspect you."

"You mean I'm not supposed to be here?"

Gopher considered. "It may be like a telepathic animal in your realm."

"Oh, you mean really different, and if anybody catches on, there could be real mischief."

"That is the case. We think concealment of your nature is best."

"Got it. I need to look normal for your realm, so there's no trouble."

"Yes. We must arrange to make you seem normal. Then we will all be all right."

"We are almost to the gully. Indigo will lead you to the cave, and watch over you."

"To make sure the bears don't get me."

"Yes. They made the deal, but they need to be reminded, because they are not truly sapient. Indigo will make sure they remember."

"That's a relief. I wasn't thinking of bears when I came here."

Gopher and Peba did the final bit of digging, and broke out to the gully wall. Now they shoved earth forward rather than back, and widened the hole until Rowan could wriggle out. She was covered with dirt, but was free of the tunnel. "Feels great to breathe fresh air again!"

"You must go immediately to the bears' cave," Gopher told her. "Sapient animals must not see you."

"Got it," she agreed. "Just show me the way."

Indigo slithered up. "Follow me," he thought.

The girl followed the snake down the gully. Gopher, relieved, turned back into the tunnel, made his way to the burrow offshoot, and went to his own cubbyhole. He was horribly tired, and needed to sleep for a day or two.

⁊⁊

He was awakened by a human scream. It was Rowan, coming awake herself. Her vision came right through to Gopher with extraordinary force. It was of a bear with blood dripping from its jaws.

"She's not attacking!" Indigo hissed. "Read her mind!"

the gopher added his reassurance to that of the snake. They bear was returning from feeding, and would now help protect their charge, as agreed.

"We made deal," the she-bear growled. She had two cubs, and planned to treat the visitor like a cub, protecting her from dangers, including other bears. The cubs were behind her, curious about the human.

Gradually the girl's alarm subsided. Indigo was connecting her mind to that of the bear, and she understood that there was no menace. The blood was from the pig the bear had just eaten, and shared with her cubs, and soon it was gone as the bear licked off her chops. She settled down beside the girl, lending her warmth in the cool cave. The cubs hesitated, then curled up with the girl.

"You're cute," Rowan thought.

Owl had not liked that thought, but the cubs did. They shared their limited minds with her, becoming friendly. One was male, the other female. The female was well behaved, but the male liked to explore. That made his mother nervous, because there were dangers out there.

Gopher tried to go back to sleep, but the girl's thoughts were too strong.

"But how could you eat a live pig?"

The mother bear considered. "Dead meat spoil. Much better fresh," she thought.

"But to tear apart a live thing!"

"What you eat?"

The girl's mind oriented on a pork chop. "Toasted dead meat," she thought.

"You burn? Ugh!"

The thoughts faded, and Gopher lapsed back into sleep. He woke some time later, feeling hungry. It wasn't his own hunger he felt, but Rowan's; she was a mammal and needed food more often than a reptile did. But it put the notion into his mind, and now he was hungry himself.

He made his way out of the burrow. The others were still resting; they were tired too. He went to the nearest grassy patch and started eating, but his mind remained on the girl. They had brought her here, but now what were they going to do with her? She was not a creature of this realm, and even though she was learning mind talk, she was not like the other animals. She wasn't like the humans here, either. There was no comfortable place for her in this world.

Gopher knew that he and the other burrow mates had acted without thinking carefully enough. They were an immature burrow, and had just proved it by doing something foolish. Yet how could they have left the girl in her own realm? Her mental affinity was closer to theirs than to her own kind in either place. So had they really had a choice?

Meanwhile the girl's thoughts continued. What was there for her to eat? "We have some raw pig left," the she-bear thought, but Rowan found that revolting.

"Humans are omnivores," Indigo thought. "Like bears. What do you eat when it's not meat?"

"Berries," the she-bear thought. "Eat."

"Berries!" Rowan agreed. "Those would be good."

"Patch near. Ripen every day in summer. We eat not today; we had pigs. I show you."

"Great!" But then she paused. "I'm not supposed to go out where sapients might see me."

"Sapients," the bear echoed with mixed feelings. "They restrict us." There was a surge of resentment.

Gopher was interested. His burrow had just made a deal with the bears that had brought them a very good meal. Why did the bears resent the sapient animals?

"I get berries," the she-bear decided. "You stay with cubs."

"But how can you pick them?" Rowan asked.

The bear pondered. "How?" she asked, stumped.

"Maybe you can knock them into a bag," Rowan thought. She made a mental picture of the process. "I have a bag." She brought out a small cloth device.

"Bag," the bear agreed, grasping the concept.

The bear took the bag in her mouth, and left the cave. Rowan stroked the cubs. They had gotten to know each other in the night, and were getting along well. The mother bear knew that, or she would never have left them with the human girl.

Gopher tuned out. The girl would have her berries, and stop being hungry. But the larger problem remained: where would she stay? What would she do? There would be trouble the moment any sapient animal not of their own burrow caught on that she was an intelligent human being, and disaster if they realized just how intelligent she was. Yet she could not remain hidden much longer in the bears' cave. She had to stay somewhere else.

The grazing wasn't good here, so Gopher moved farther from the burrow. He checked the minds of other sapients within range; there was no mischief nearby. He found some tasty low leaves, and snapped them up avidly. It was good to be eating properly again.

Then a sapient mind approached at a moderate pace. It was not local. A raccoon on a howdah, traveling through this area on the way to a distant burrow. Gopher expanded his mind, letting the raccoon know of his presence.

In due course a male human tramped into sight. The howdah was a wooden framework attached to his shoulders and sitting above his head. The raccoon perched on it just above the head, gazing forward.

The human halted, obeying a mental command. The raccoon gazed down at Gopher. "Greeting, Tortoise."

"Greeting, Raccoon."

"Is this your territory?"

"My burrow is not yet sanctioned. The territory is

open."

"Then I will forage here." The human squatted, then sat on the ground, so that the raccoon could conveniently jump down. It was a routine maneuver.

Gopher was annoyed that he had been unable to reserve this territory for their own burrow. But he couldn't, until their burrow was complete and recognized. He couldn't even travel in style, the way the raccoon was, on the howdah.

And then he had an inspiration. He closed his mind, not wishing to share his notion with a stranger. "I will return to my burrow. Good foraging."

"Thank you." The raccoon disappeared into the brush, while the human male sat waiting, his thoughts dull.

Gopher hurried home, keeping his thoughts muted until he was out of range of the raccoon. Only when he was in the burrow did he let his mind reach out to the others. "Burrow gathering tonight."

They were there when the evening came, all of them fairly rested after a day of sleep. They could tell it was important, because of Gopher's excitement. "This concerns the girl," Indigo thought, and of course he wasn't guessing. "She is sleeping now; need I wake her?"

"No need," Gopher replied. "Only if my idea is good."

"We do have a problem," Owl thought. "I don't know why I didn't get an overview of it before."

"Because you like the girl, you feathered curmudgeon," Cottontail thought. "As do we all. We weren't thinking of problems, we just wanted her with us."

"We're an immature burrow," Peba thought. "We need more maturity, and a better mind."

"Too bad that raccoon was taken," Gopher thought. "He was a sensible one, but he was traveling to join another burrow." Then he launched into his encounter with the raccoon. "And when I saw the dull human man sitting there, I realized that Rowan could do that."

"She's not dull," Indigo thought. "That's the problem."

"But she's human. She can *seem* dull. No one will suspect."

"I must object," Indigo thought. "This girl has the finest mind we have encountered. To make her become a dull beast of burden—that would be an outrage, even if she is technically human."

"She can *seem* dull," Gopher repeated. "Not *be* dull. She can be among us, unchallenged, as our bearer, and see our whole society. We alone will know her true nature. She will have freedom, as long as she pretends to be dull. Just as we were all right in the other realm as long as none of the natives knew we were telepathic."

They pondered this. "Tortoise, this is a remarkable idea," Owl thought. "I am surprised you thought of it."

"It was just chance. I saw the raccoon foraging in our territory, and the dull human bearer, and Rowan was on my mind, and it came to me. I couldn't even be sure it was a good idea. I had to share it with the burrow."

They considered it. "I believe it is good," Indigo thought. "If she agrees."

There was a mental murmur of agreement from the others. Gopher's idea had passed muster. He was pleased, for it was rare that he was able to do original thinking; it wasn't his nature.

"However, there remains a problem," Indigo thought, as usual coming up with the odd aspect. "She can't remain long here in the bear's cave. In time they will get hungry again, and she is young and tasty. She must have a secure residence of her own, and she will not fit in the burrow."

"Humans don't normally live in burrows anyway," Owl thought. "Just as most birds don't."

"Sensible birds live in trees," Cottontail thought, and there was friendly humor from the others.

"Could she live in a tree?" Owl asked.

That was an interesting notion, and they focused on it. "Humans can climb trees, if they think of it," Gopher agreed.

"But mostly they live in crude shelters on the ground," Peba thought. "To keep the rain off and the flies out."

"And sometimes hungry creatures get at them," Indigo thought. "They might be better off in trees."

"Maybe if Rowan agrees," Gopher thought. He always tried to achieve unity in the burrow, and this was a burrow matter.

"Maybe now is the time to wake her," Cottontail thought. "We need to know how she feels about this."

There was a pause as Indigo focused on the human girl, who was sleeping with the two cubs. Gopher felt her come awake. There was confusion as she oriented on the snake's mental question.

Then her reaction came. "A treehouse! Great!"

She liked the notion! "Now ask her about the bearer," Gopher thought. That was really more important.

There was another pause as the girl assimilated the notion. "This way I can be with you?" she asked. "With all of you, without hiding?"

"Only your mind," Indigo thought. "Other sapients must not know you are smart. You must pretend to be dull. Only we burrow mates must know your mental power."

"Sure. You're the only folk I care about anyway. I knew there'd be problems for me here, just as there are for you in my realm. I can play the game, if it means I can stay here without trouble."

"We believe that is what it means," Gopher thought. "We feel you should have some experience of our realm before you decide to remain here."

"That makes sense. But there's nothing for me back in my own world, so I'd better like it here. I know I will, as long as I'm with you folk of the burrow." But there was an undercurrent of regret; Gopher realized that it was not entirely easy for her to leave the realm she had known all her life. She might have serious doubts, once she realized just how different things were here.

But he did not think that to her. "We will arrange for a howdah, and see what we can do with the nearest tree to the burrow. Sleep with the bears tonight, and we will find another place for you in the morning."

"Good enough. Mama Bear is okay, once you get to know her. She treats me like a cub." She stroked the cubs, who liked her touch. They had become good friends.

"That is her way." But Gopher did not add that this was safe only while the bears were not hungry. The mother bear would protect her cubs against all threats without limit, but Rowan was not a cub, however it might seem at the moment. They needed to get her out of the bear cave before the other bears got any awkward notions. "Then it is decided; tomorrow we will act."

"Tomorrow, the new world," Rowan agreed.

Gopher hoped it would be that easy.

Chapter 9
Treehouse

Rowan was ready at dawn. Indigo had alerted her, and she had eaten more berries and straightened herself out as well as she could. "I must look a sight," she thought. "I haven't been able to wash in two days."

"We will take you to a stream," Indigo replied. He understood from her mind that she really did prefer to be clean, unlike regular humans. "Now we must go to join the burrow mates."

"Bye, Mama Bear," she said to the bear who had been her companion for the past day and night. On occasion one of the others had looked toward her, licking chops, but Mama Bear had growled warningly, making them back off. It was clear enough; she needed to get out of here before they got any hungrier. Indigo could have stopped a bear if he had to, with a mind blast relayed from her mind, but preferred to keep things amicable if possible. She understood and agreed: they might need to exchange favors again some time.

They left the cave and walked to the mouth of the burrow. The others were there: Gopher Tortoise, Burrowing Owl, Peba Armadillo, and Cottontail Rabbit. She was glad to see them all again, though she had been in mind touch all along.

"Oh, I could just hug all of you!" she exclaimed.

"Do not do this," Owl thought gruffly.

"Peba and I do not hug well," Gopher thought.

"Hug me," Cottontail thought. "Except for my leg."

Rowan bent down, picked the rabbit up carefully, and hugged him gently. "I should carry you anyway, until your leg is better." She set him on her shoulder.

"We must get you a howdah, so you can carry any of us," Gopher thought. "So no one will suspect your nature."

"That's right: I've got to play stupid. I can do that."

"Carry me also," Gopher thought. "Follow Peba."

She made a place in one of her bags, and set the tortoise in it. Then she walked after the armadillo, who scooted along a path through the forest. Owl took off and soon disappeared, and Indigo was gone in the brush.

They came to a stream. "Here you can wash," Gopher thought.

"Oh, good!" She set down the bag, put Cottontail down, and got out of her clothing. She waded into the stream. "Ooo, it's cold!"

"We can numb you to the cold," Cottontail thought.

"You can? Make me so I can't feel it? Okay, since I've got to wash anyway, I might as well be comfortable. Do it."

Then the water around her calves seemed to warm. The stream was only knee deep, but flowing firmly. She squatted, then sat, and it was like a lukewarm bath. This was weird!

She splashed water all over herself, and saw the grime soiling the river and being borne away. She dipped her hair in it, rinsing out more dirt. That long crawl through the tunnel had really coated her body.

When she was clean, she brought her filthy clothing in with her and rinsed it out as well as she could. "But it will be hours before I can wear this again," she thought.

"You will wear the bearer costume," Indigo thought, appearing from the brush. "So it is better you go unclothed, lest your unusual apparel arouse suspicion."

"That's right! I didn't think of that. It's a good thing the bears didn't catch on."

"The bears are not fully sapient," Gopher reminded her. "The raccoons are."

Rowan emerged from the stream, trying to shake herself dry. "We're going to see raccoons?"

"They have the howdah," Gopher thought.

"Okay. I feel funny walking outside naked, but I guess it won't be for long."

"Not for long," Gopher agreed.

She hung her wet clothing up on bushes to dry, knowing she could return for them later. She still felt comfortable, but saw goose pimples on her arms and legs, so knew she was really cold. The animals kept coming up with mind tricks she had never thought of.

"It is part of being sapient," Cottontail explained. "At times we need to keep ourselves or our bearers comfortable when the weather is wrong."

They moved on beyond the stream. Rowan felt her body warming as she walked; the air was not cold, just the water, and after a while she no longer needed the numbing. That was a relief, because she did not want to mistreat her body.

They came to a stone structure like a wall. A raccoon sat on it. "What do you offer, burrower?" his thought came. He was directing it to Gopher, but the tortoise was sharing it with Rowan.

Gopher poked his head out of the bag. "A secret."

"We have many secrets already."

"This one is rare, known only to our burrow."

The raccoon peered down at the tortoise. "What you think is rare may not seem so to us."

"We will let you judge. If you find it worthy, you will set our human bearer up with costume and howdah. You will not reveal it beyond your group."

The raccoon looked at Rowan with disconcerting appraisal. She felt his mind probing hers, and immediately dumbed down her thoughts. This creature was smarter than any of the borrow-mates! "We can do this. What is your secret?"

Gopher addressed Rowan. "Open your mind to him, with your origin strongest."

Oh. She reversed course, and opened her mind, thinking of her home realm and their recent crawl through the tunnel.

The raccoon fell off the wall.

Rowan laughed. She couldn't help it.

The raccoon climbed back onto the wall. "May we see the portal?"

"I will take you there," Peba thought.

"Deal accepted." The raccoon glanced at Rowan again. "Go with our kind." Then he bounded off the wall and followed Peba back along the path.

Another raccoon appeared on the wall. "Come with me," she thought. Rowan could not tell male from female by appearance, but the mind was definitely feminine.

"Go with her," Gopher thought. "We will wait here."

Rowan closed most of her mind, then stepped up to the wall, and over it, following the raccoon. In a moment they came to a cloth costume hanging from a branch. It was dull brown, resembling a parka. "Don this."

Rowan took the parka and put it on. It fell comfortably around her, with holes for her arms and a hood for her head, reaching to her knees. The raccoons must have known she was coming, because this had been set out for her.

"I like it," she said.

The lady raccoon was startled. "You really do vocalize!"

"Oops—I'm not supposed to do that here. I'll try to keep my mouth shut."

"And you really are sapient!"

"Yes, incredibly," Rowan agreed, amused.

"We have never before encountered a sapient human animal. How is this possible?"

"In my realm, humans are smart and animals are stupid," Rowan explained. "And no one has telepathy."

"Amazing! The tortoise was right: this is a truly worthy secret." She looked at Rowan again. "*All* humans are sapient in your realm?"

"Yes. And no animals. It's topsy turvy."

The raccoon got her meaning from her mind. "It is. I see why the burrow denizens want to conceal your nature. There would be alarm if it were generally known."

"Just as there would be in my realm, if people learned of smart telepathic animals. So we kept the secret there, and will keep it here."

"And no raccoon will reveal it." The lady paused. "If you should ever need other refuge, come to us. We are the smartest animal, and value intelligence. I see that you are even smarter than we are."

"I didn't say that," Rowan protested, not wanting to upset the creature.

"When you opened your mind to us, we saw. The rest of us did not really believe it, but now we do. You are the smartest creature in this realm."

"I'm just an ordinary human girl. I don't even make top grades."

"In your own realm. We must see that others of your kind do not come here. It would be dangerous to us."

"Maybe not. I'm the only one who is telepathic, and I'm not very good at it."

The raccoon considered. "Yes, this makes a difference. But it is still better that your kind does not come here; it would be severely disruptive."

"That's what I think. I want me to be the only one. And it's not safe for your kind in my realm."

"True. Now come to the howdah."

Rowan followed the lady raccoon to another wall. There sat an object like a huge helmet made of wooden spokes, with a flat platform above, surrounded by a rail and covered by a cloth canopy. It looked cumbersome. "I'm supposed to wear that?"

"It is more comfortable than it seems, and it will conceal your nature completely. Set it over your head, on your shoulders."

Rowan was dubious, but she picked up the contraption. It was much lighter than it looked, as the wood struts were thin and so was the platform. She lifted it over her head, then brought it slowly down until the supports touched her shoulders. They had padded U-shaped ends that fit around her shoulder bones and held the main part of it upright. The platform was just over her head, not touching it, so she could look around or down without disturbing it. "I feel like an alien from Mars!"

"You feel strange," the raccoon agreed, not comprehending much of the reference. "But you will get used to it. No sapient creature will pay any attention to you as long as you wear the howdah and keep your mind closed. This is how it protects you. Now squat low so I can conveniently board."

Rowan slowly squatted, until the platform was almost level with the top of the wall. The raccoon jumped to it. "Now rise slowly. A good bearer never shakes up the riders."

Rowan stood as smoothly as she could. She could not see the raccoon now, but could feel her weight on her shoulders. It was bearable.

"Now follow the path back to where the tortoise waits. Make your face dull. You may look around, so as to see your way clearly, but do not show any real interest in others."

"I'm stupid," Rowan agreed. "Duh."

"Keep your mind closed," the raccoon reminded her. "That will betray your nature fastest of all. Tune in only to your rider. Only when you are alone may you reach out with your mind."

"Got it." Rowan walked slowly back along the path, concentrating on keeping the howdah level and unshaken.

"That is good. You will learn to walk very smoothly, and never misstep. When you encounter other human beings, ignore them. You have interest only in your rider. That is the way of the bearer."

"Right." Rowan would have been annoyed, but realized that this was indeed her best concealment. If she acted dumb and kept her mind closed, she would seem just like a beast of burden. No sapient animal would ever suspect her of being smart.

They came to the first wall. "Squat low," the raccoon thought.

Rowan squatted, and the raccoon jumped from the howdah to the top of the wall. "Here is your bearer," she thought to the burrow mates. "We have fulfilled our part of the bargain."

"And we have fulfilled ours," Gopher thought. "We have shown you our secret, and your representative is down in our burrow seeing it for himself."

"We have offered your alien human sanctuary if she ever needs it."

"She will not need if it she remains concealed." Then Gopher sent a thought directly to Rowan. "Pick me up. Put me on the howdah."

"Yes, massa," Rowan thought. She reached down, picked him up, and lifted him to the platform over her head. She set him down somewhat awkwardly, because the canopy and little railing got in the way.

"We must practice that," Gopher thought. "Now rise."

She stood up. Now the tortoise was over her head, out of her sight, but his mind made it quite clear he was there.

"Our business is done," the lady raccoon thought, and jumped off the wall, disappearing into the brush.

"Now get down and put Cottontail on the howdah," Gopher thought.

Rowan did so, making a better job of it this time, though she felt a twinge from the rabbit's hurt leg. The howdah transferred the weight directly to her shoulders, and it wasn't bad. No worse than a knapsack.

"Follow Indigo," Gopher thought.

She saw the snake slither onto the path. She walked after him. He moved at a brisk pace. She made sure to walk evenly, so as not to shake up the howdah, and knew she was getting better as she went. Then she picked up her bags and carried them with her free hands. The howdah did make it easier to carry both animals and bags.

"Is it okay to talk now?"

"As long as no sapient animal is close," Gopher agreed.

"How come neither you nor the raccoon said thank you?"

"This is a concept relevant to your realm rather than ours. We know each other's minds, so are satisfied with formal agreement that the terms of a deal have been met."

"I guess that makes sense. We non-telepaths need to state more things openly."

They reached the burrow. She tucked her bags into a nook formed by a low branch of the tree near it, then resumed walking in a new direction. Indigo remained at the burrow, and so did Cottontail, so now she was alone with Gopher.

They came to a fork in the path. Rowan took the right fork without even thinking to inquire, though it was new to her. Then she realized that Gopher had directed her, so that she knew without having to ask. That was the way it was, with a bearer.

They came to a region of the forest where there were a number of dead trees. She collected several dry bare branches and carried them in her arms. They were heavy, but she could manage. She took them to the tree beside the burrow.

Their next trip was to fetch some strong grape vines. These had died the season before, but remained hanging from trees. She had to set down the howdah, climb up those trees, and use her pocket knife to cut them from the top, because even dead they would not let go. She got a number of long rope-like stretches that were flexible enough to serve.

"Now we must fetch something from below," Gopher thought. Peba had returned by this time, having shown the raccoon the deepest depth of the tunnel to the other realm. He disappeared into the burrow, and returned hauling a bundle of stringy roots. They put these in one of Rowan's bags, and she carried it with her.

Then they traveled to a tree where several birds were supervising dull humans in weaving cloth. She did not recognize the species, so thought of them as weaver birds. The birds knew how to make secure nests, and could tell when a piece was proper; the humans had the finger dexterity to do it, when properly directed. Of course the burrow had to make a deal, and in this case Gopher proffered a special kind of root that was found mainly in lightless caves. Tortoise burrows had access to such caves, but most birds did not; Owl's loyalty was to the burrow, so he would not provide such roots for other birds unless in trade for something the burrow needed. The birds needed the roots for special types of cloth. They were a standard trading item for any burrow. Rowan opened her bag and brought out the bundle of roots, and the deal was made. The roots didn't look special, but the birds knew what was what, and these were the right type.

Rowan couldn't help noticing the humans, covertly. They were adult men and woman, wearing parkas of different dull colors, and their expressions were moronic. They seemed to have no interest in anything but what their hands were working on. She tried to feel their minds a little, but all she found was dullness. They were not very clean, physically, either; they did not seem to care that they were dirty. The hair of both males and females grew dully down their backs. In fact there was not much to distinguish the genders; the men were not handsome, the women not attractive. She did not like them at all. It was true: the human beings of this realm were stupid.

"They are not your kind," Gopher thought when they were alone again.

"They sure aren't!" She had known it, but not fully believed it; now she believed. She had far more in common with the animals of this realm than with the humans, despite her human body. "Maybe I should get dirty again, so my cleanness doesn't give me away."

"No need. Different animals have different preferences, and different types of labor have different standards. Some riders prefer to ride in style, with everything clean. We can be that type, if you wish. The humans you saw were not bearers, but workers; it doesn't matter how they look, as long as they work well."

"I do wish. I was never much for fancy clothing, but I've always been clean. It's healthier."

"We will have a healthy bearer," Gopher agreed.

Now she had the materials to make her tree house. She set Gopher on the ground and removed the howdah. It was a relief; it had not been too heavy, but she wasn't used to it, and her shoulders and back were getting tired.

"This is something you must do for yourself," Gopher thought. "We are not clever with trees or above-ground construction. But you should be able to fashion something suitable, and we can get other supplies you need for it."

"Thanks; I'll be fine," she thought. "I'll climb this tree and find the best place for my treehouse, and make it. I'm not used to vines instead of a hammer and nails, but I'll make do."

"I will graze," Gopher thought. He departed.

Rowan climbed the tree. It was a good-sized live oak, with considerable foliage, and a number of big gnarley branches extending outward and upward. She found a place where three branches diverged, forming a solid pocket that was hard to see from the ground. She used the vines to tie the dead branches she had brought to the live ones, making sure they were secure, forming crude walls. Then she hung cloth on them to make them windproof. Her house was cup-shaped rather than square, but she thought it would do.

Except for one thing: it had no roof. Oh, the canopy of the higher foliage closed it off from the sky, but she knew that when rain came, she would get soaked. That would never do. She had to have something waterproof overhead.

"I've got a problem," she thought to Gopher, reaching out for his mind.

"Need I return to the burrow?" His thought was faint; he was grazing some distance away.

"No. I just hope you have the answer. I need a roof. Something to keep the rain out of my treehouse."

"I did not think of that," Gopher thought. "The burrow does not need a roof. The birds also make waterproof material that some humans use for their shelters. Some use nothing but this material, strung on poles."

"Tents!" Rowan thought. "Tight canvas. That would do."

"We must go back to the birds to make another trade. But this type of cloth is special, so they require more for it."

"I was afraid of something like that. Can we get it?"

"Yes. But it will take more time."

It turned out that there was a special type of fungus

that grew only in the deepest, wettest caves, that glowed with different colors. The birds used it to make glowing cloths that were quite rare. Because Gopher was an unusually curious tortoise—most tortoises soon settled into routine, but he was unreformed—he had discovered such a cave and knew where it was. But the fungus had to be harvested fresh, and there was never very much of it at a time. They would have to make a special excursion to that cave and glean what they could.

Fortunately it was near the deep tunnel that went to the other realm. So Gopher and Peba widened the passage to it, and Rowan joined them for the harvest. It was beautiful; the fungus glowed all around it, mostly green, but some was blue, and some red. It was like a fairyland. "I almost hate to take this," she thought. "It's so lovely as it is, I don't like spoiling it."

The others picked up the idea of beauty from her mind. "It *is* lovely," Peba agreed. "I never knew that concept before."

They harvested it carefully, scraping the fungus off the walls of the cave, leaving some of each color so that it would grow again. Rowan put the scrapings into her bag. By the time they were done, it was night, and she was hungry. She had had nothing to eat but berries in the bears' cave.

"We feel your hunger," Peba thought. "We must get food for you."

"It would help," Rowan thought. "I've been distracted all day, making the tree house and all, but I do need to eat."

"We can get you regular vegetables," Gopher thought. "Go with Owl."

They crawled out of the cave and the burrow. Owl was there. He flew across to perch on Rowan's shoulder. "This way."

She followed his mind, seeing more clearly in the darkness. They came to a den where a fox stood.

"We need to trade," Owl thought to the fox.

"What is your range?"

"It is not official, for we are not yet recognized as a

burrow, but no one has challenged it." Owl opened his mind to show an aerial view of the region of their burrow.

"It will do," the fox thought. "Do we have exclusive hunting privileges, apart from your burrow members?"

"We can't guarantee that, but if no one challenges, you will have it."

"Understood." The fox gazed at Rowan. "You have a hungry human female."

"She is young, so may eat less than a grown one."

"True. And there is something about her mind that intrigues me."

Rowan quickly damped down her thoughts; she had to learn to be careful all the time. The raccoons claimed to be the smartest animals, but she suspected the foxes were. She let slip only thoughts of stupidity.

"Perhaps not," the fox concluded. "She may use my garden for herself alone, as long as I have good hunting in your territory."

"Agreed." Owl oriented on Rowan. "I will show you the garden. Take only what you need."

The fox disappeared, evidently to hunt in the burrow's territory. Rowan walked where Owl indicated, using his good night vision, and found a roughly planted vegetable garden. She recognized carrots, turnips, squash, lettuce, tomatoes, peppers, and potatoes. She had never been much for salads, but suddenly these looked very good. "Can I cook any of this?"

"Yes, if you have fire."

"Maybe tomorrow. Right now I'll settle for the vegetables I can eat raw." She plucked several big red tomatoes and put them in her bag. Then she pulled some carrots and carefully tore off several lettuce leaves.

"The fox also has fruit," Owl thought.

She looked where his mind indicated, and saw strawberries, blueberries, and raspberries. They looked wonderful. She picked a number, eating them as she picked. "This is great!"

Then they made their way back to the burrow, using Owl's good night vision. "I wish I could see as you do," she thought wistfully. "With my own eyes, I mean."

"There is no need. I will share whenever you need."

"Yes. That's the great thing about the burrow. You burrow mates share, and it makes you all better than you are alone."

"Still, I would like to be able to think as you do," Owl thought. "Sharing your mind is like flying over the sun."

"I'll always share when you need it," she thought.

"And, sharing you mind, I see the irony," Owl thought. "We each envy the other, yet each sees no need for the other to envy. That concept is well beyond my isolated mind, but makes wonderful sense with yours."

"I love sharing with all of you. You're—you're *company*, in the best sense. It's impossible to be lonely when you're with nice other minds. This telepathy—it's so much more than just talking without my mouth. I get the full context, including your feelings. I know you didn't like me at first, but now you do."

"Now I do," Owl agreed. "Now you have seen the humans of this realm, so you understand my prejudice."

"Yes. Humans are such brutes." She paused. "In my realm, too, many of them. Mind sharing is not only better, it's nicer. No one deceives anyone."

"Actually deception is possible. But it requires practice and concentration, and we are not good at it."

She laughed. "I'm better at it, because it happens all the time in my realm. But I never want to lie to any of you."

They reached the burrow and the tree. "We do not have your waterproof cloth tonight," Owl thought. "But there is no cloud in the sky, so you will not be wet."

"One other thing I still need. I've got potatoes, but I can't eat them raw. I need fire to cook them."

"Tomorrow we will get you fire," Owl thought.

"Okay. These other vegetables and fruits will do tonight. So I'm set for the night, I guess. And you have to hunt; I feel it in your mind. You're trying to be nice and not desert me, but as you said, you aren't good at deception. Go hunt, Owl; I'll be fine."

Without further thought, Owl spread his wings and took off into the night sky. Soon his thoughts were fading with distance.

Rowan wiped off a carrot and bit into it. She would have preferred to wash it, but had no water. She was lucky the fruits were juicy, so she wasn't thirsty. She'd see about getting a pail so she could have clean water in her treehouse. Right now she was tired; it had been a long day.

She climbed the tree and got into her tree-cup. She'd need to get a pillow, too, and a blanket, so she wouldn't have to use her parka to sleep in. So there were things to be done. Tomorrow, or the day after. Right now she would make do.

She curled up in the bottom of the cup and closed her eyes. And heard the mosquitoes. They had not been bold while she was active, but now they swarmed—and she had no repellant.

"We're going to suck your blood," the mosquitoes thought faintly. They did not actually think in a sentence, but that was the essence. Their hollow noses were quivering for her tender flesh.

Rowan was fed up with nuisances. "If you do, I'll blow you into oblivion!" she thought fiercely, forming a mental picture of a grenade exploding, sending bits of bugs out in a grisly shower.

Suddenly the swarm was gone.

"What do you know! I scared them off." She realized that telepathy had yet another use. It seemed that all creatures of this realm were telepathic, at least to some degree, and responsive to the minds of others. She could make friends by being mentally pleasant—and could drive away others by being mentally nasty. That was a useful discovery.

She established a background thought of stinky mosquito repellent, and drifted to sleep.

Chapter 10
Threat

Cottontail's leg was healing, but he still could not run well. That would be dangerous out in the field. So he joined Rowan, amplifying her contact with the others and answering her questions, while she took him to the river and grazing field. Actually one of them had to be with her, by day, to ride in the howdah, so that the human girl seemed legitimate. He was the one, this day.

First they went to the closest stream, where they drank, and then Rowan removed her parka and washed her body. Cottontail didn't fully understand why she did that, but realized that it wasn't easy for her to clean her body by licking it all over. He helped her by making her not feel the cold, and tried to show her how she could do that for herself. A mind could do a lot, when it knew how. Then they went to the grazing field, when he dismounted and feasted on the best leaves.

Now there was the matter of the roof for her treehouse. Cottontail understood why she didn't want to get rained on; dry was generally more comfortable. Owl joined them for this, as it was easier for a bird to deal with other birds.

They took the bag of glowing fungus to the weaving birds. The organization of birds was not the same as a burrow, but several kinds often shared a particular tree for sleeping and nesting, and considered themselves tree mates. Only the larger birds were fully sapient, like the hawks, the owls, the largest woodpeckers, the turkeys, and the herons, but smaller ones shared to an extent.

They came to a large magnolia tree, where the birds they wanted perched on low branches. "We have glow fungus," Owl announced. "We want rainproof cloth."

A red-shouldered hawk inspected the open bag Rowan held up. "It will do," he thought.

On a branch on the far side of the tree hung a broad length of heavy cloth. "Canvas!" Rowan thought, delighted.

The hawk peered down at her disapprovingly. "Your bearer is expressive."

"She likes pretty things," Owl explained, while Rowan quickly shut down her thoughts. She still tended to forget to keep her mind closed.

"This is not pretty, it is functional," the hawk thought.

"It is pretty to her simple human mind."

Cottontail felt Rowan's effort to suppress her laughter. But it was a good explanation; the hawk lost interest in the human. Rowan lifted the heavy cloth with her arms and carried it back to the burrow. She piled it into her treehouse.

Next they attended to the girl's need for fire. "Take along a pole," Cottontail advised.

"We'll be trading a pole for fire?"

"Not exactly." He tried to clarify the concept, but bungled it.

"I'm sure I'll find out soon enough," she thought.

They went by the region of dead trees, and Rowan searched until she found a piece that would serve as a staff, about as tall as she was, strong, and not too heavy. Cottontail had her strike tree trunks with it as she passed, and to tap hard on rocks. She needed to be able to use it efficiently.

"Why?" she inquired.

"To protect yourself and your rider the way humans do. We will try to trade protection for fire." He shared his thought with her. This time he got it right.

"Maybe that will work," she agreed. "But I think we'll need to make a demonstration."

This was another new concept. Cottontail discussed

it with her, and came to understand her reasoning. "Yes, this is better."

He brought her back toward the burrow. Near it was an opossum, poking around and under the dry leaves of the forest floor. "Hail, Possum!" Cottontail thought from the howdah platform.

The possum paused, gazing up at the rabbit. "What do you want with me?"

"Fire."

"I have it. What do you offer?"

"Tolerance by the burrow."

"The only burrow mate I fear is the indigo snake, and he has never hunted me."

"Because we thought we might one day need your fire. Now we do."

"None of you use fire."

"But our new bearer does."

The opossum looked directly at Rowan for the first time. "That's yours? I thought you borrowed it."

"She is ours. We are maintaining her. We need fire to cook her food."

"Tolerance isn't enough. There are other threats."

"Protection, then."

"How can you protect me from a coyote or a wildcat? I see by your mind you were injured by a cat."

"I was. Now I have protection."

"In a howdah. But I forage on the ground."

"Let us imagine," Cottontail thought. "Let's call that rock there a wildcat ready to pounce. Bearer: strike it!"

Rowan understood his ploy, because she had devised it. She strode toward the rock, swinging her pole at it. There was a thud as it struck. Then she jammed the end of the pole into the rock, rolling it over.

"That wildcat is hurting," Cottontail thought to the opossum.

The possum was impressed. "But would she help me when I need it?"

"If we make the deal, you must attune your mind to hers, so that she can hear your call for help. Then she will come as quickly as she can, with her pole. You will have to give her time to come, but if you do, she should be able to drive off your attacker."

The opossum addressed Rowan. "Do you hear me, human?"

"Yes. I will come when you call, with my pole."

The possum was taken aback. "You feel sapient!"

Oops. Cottontail realized that he should have cautioned her to respond stupidly, keeping her mind mostly closed.

But the girl had an answer. "The burrow mates require me to communicate like them. They don't like stupid humans."

The possum was not fully convinced. "Most humans are unable to do that. They *are* stupid."

"I am smart for a human. If you do not think anything complicated at me, I can manage to seem almost sapient."

That persuaded the opossum. "I will make this deal," he thought to Cottontail.

"Give us fire."

The opossum rummaged in some brush, and brought out a small clay pot filled with dry leaf fragments. "Here is a fire-pot. Do you know how to use it?"

"Not well," Cottontail thought. "See if you can make the human girl understand."

The opossum used a foreclaw to scrape away part of the leaf mixture. A tiny curl of smoke rose from the pot. "Touch a dry leaf or straw to the inside, and breathe on it to make the flame come. Follow my mind."

Rowan lifted the pot, took a dry stem of grass, and followed the opossum's mental instructions. She poked the stem in and blew on it, not too hard. In a moment the pot glowed and the stem caught fire.

"Do it that way," the opossum concluded. "The coals in the pot will last several days, if you keep them dry. When they burn out, and you need fire again, bring the pot to me and I will give you another."

Cottontail saw that the girl already understood the principle very well, having worked with fire before. She could repack the pot to keep the coals alive much longer.

But that would give away her intelligence. "We will do that," he agreed. "Meanwhile, when you are ready, send the human a call, to be sure she receives you. Then you will know you have protection."

"I will do that," the possum agreed.

They returned to the burrow. "How come possums have fire?" Rowan asked him.

"They do it for trade, the same as the raccoons, fox, and birds. We are a trading society. Many animals have specialties, and it is easier to deal with them than to try to do all things ourselves."

"I like it. I always thought possums were pretty stupid."

"In your realm they surely are. Here they are sapient."

"That's right. I keep forgetting. But why is it that only animals in your size range are sapient? I can see why the smaller ones are duller, because they just don't have enough brain. But what about the bears and humans?"

"We don't know. We think it is that the larger creatures have enough physical power to be out of danger from most other animals, so never needed to get very smart. But we are not sure."

"Maybe some day I'll figure it out."

They were back at the tree. Cottontail dismounted, and the girl took off the howdah and set it and her staff carefully beside the tree. Then Rowan gathered twigs and dry leaves, used the fire-pot as directed, and soon had a small fire burning. She buried her potatoes in the ground beside it, then moved the fire so that it burned right above them. She did indeed know what she was doing.

"Human! Come quickly!" It was the opossum's practice call.

"Go alone!" Cottontail thought.

"Got it." She grabbed the pole and ran toward the summons.

Cottontail sat by the fire. He had never been much for such a thing, but seeing how the girl used it impressed him. It made it possible for her to eat things she could not otherwise digest. He wondered what baked potato tasted like.

Gopher emerged from the burrow and joined him. "She has fire."

"We made the deal. Now she is protecting the opossum."

"That is good. I hope our association with her is worthwhile."

"You have doubt?"

"We have used up most of our resources in order to maintain her. Our hunting range, our special roots, our glowing fungus, and now we must protect the opossum. This is a burden."

"But her mind," Cottontail thought. "There is nothing else like it."

"Yes. But are we being foolish, because we like her mind so much? We have made no progress in getting recognized as an established burrow. When winter comes and foraging grows harder, we may regret it."

"You have thought this through farther than I have."

"It is my business, as burrow landlord. And association with her mind has enabled me to think much more clearly."

Cottontail struggled with a concept. "She would call that—irony. Association with her makes us understand that maybe we shouldn't associate with her."

"Yes. But we want it as much as she does."

"We shall have to establish our burrow," Cottontail agreed. "We have been foolish, but I would not send the girl away. There must be a way to use that fantastic mind of hers for more than just the pleasure of larger understanding."

"I hope so."

Then Owl flew down and landed on the lowest branch of the tree. "We have a problem."

In a moment they had it from his mind: he had been hunting near a hawk, and exchanged thoughts. The hawk was part of a predatory female burrow that was looking for a better territory to move into. The hawk had gotten the description of Owl's burrow from his mind before he realized what she was up to, and she had concluded that this was a good region. Especially since the existing burrow was not formally recognized. That meant it was open territory; as an established burrow they could simple displace the local one and stake claim to the territory.

"This is disaster!" Gopher thought.

"If only I had masked the fact that we are not yet recognized," Owl thought. "But I didn't think to, and I fear the hawk would have had it from me anyway; she is adult, and has a sharper mind and more experience."

"We must have a burrow meeting," Gopher thought.

"Yes. But I think there is nothing we can do."

Rowan returned. "The possum is satisfied," she thought. "I got there quickly and knocked over another rock." Then she looked for carefully at the three of them. "What's the matter? Your minds are shaken up."

"A rival burrow may oust us," Cottontail explained.

"Burrows do that? I thought they respected each other's territories."

"They do," Cottontail agreed. "But we are not yet a recognized burrow. We have not yet gotten our sixth sapient member, or applied for approval by the Council of Tortoises."

"But you're a rabbit. Why would you have to apply to the tortoises?"

"It is a tortoise burrow," Gopher explained. "I am the one who must apply. I need five other sapients of suitable character and competence. Because I am a young, unreformed tortoise, I must demonstrate mature responsibility, and my resident sapients must be especially apt. We had hoped for a raccoon, but not yet found one who is interested. So we are an informal burrow, and as such have no territorial rights. Any established burrow could take over our territory if it wanted to."

"But can't you resist? I mean, stop them physically from moving in? Or isn't that the way you work."

"It is not the way we work," Owl thought. "But even it it were, we could not compete against this burrow. It has five hunters; all its residents are grown female predators."

"Female? There are male and female burrows?"

"They don't have to be," Cottontail thought. "We happen to be all male, because we are all young impetuous animals, and most females don't like that. But some burrows are mixed. If a female raccoon wanted to join us, we would welcome her."

"So what are these formidable predators?" Rowan asked.

"A hawk," Owl thought. "A rattlesnake. A civet cat, wildcat, and coyote."

Rowan leaned her back against the trunk of the tree. "I see what you mean. Those are some mean brutes."

"Not mean, merely mature—and formidable," Cottontail thought. "Any of them could make a meal of me."

"We shall hold a burrow meeting when Indigo and Peba return," Gopher thought. "To consider our best course."

"Can I sit in?" Rowan asked. "I mean, I've been a lot of trouble to all of you, and maybe I can help in some way."

"It will take more than a stick to beat back these creatures," Cottontail thought.

"Even if I can't help, I'd like to listen in. If my going back to my own realm would solve your problem, I'd do that, though I love it here."

"This problem would have come regardless," Owl thought. "It is not your fault."

"You may sit in," Gopher decided. "Meanwhile, we should rest and consider what we might do."

Gopher and Owl entered the burrow, leaving Cottontail with Rowan. "I know you don't want to go back," he thought. "But if we can't maintain a viable burrow, you may have to, because others would not accept you here."

"You're right. If you have to move, it would be all you could do just to survive. And I couldn't use this treehouse, after all our effort to make it possible."

Cottontail knew from her mind that she was very unhappy about the prospect. In fact she was close to crying. That wasn't a thing that rabbits did, but her sadness infused his mind and made him want to. "Perhaps you could go with the raccoons," he suggested.

"I don't *want* to be with the raccoons. I want to be

with you."

He liked that, without fully understanding why.

They held the burrow meeting in the afternoon, at the mouth of the burrow, with Rowan tuning in from the tree. Gopher reviewed the situation for Indigo and Peba. "Now we must decide what to do," he concluded.

"There is no chance to reason with them?" Peba asked. "We may not yet be recognized by the tortoises, but we are functioning as a burrow, and of course every burrow has to start at some time. All were new once. Would they recognize our right to this territory?"

"They are predators," Owl responded. "They have an aggressive attitude. They might accept my rights, and Indigo's, but they would simply want to eat Cottontail."

That made Cottontail jump, evoking a twinge in his leg. It was true: four or five of the six members of that burrow would regard him as prey. "Could the rest of you make a physical stand if I departed?" he asked.

"No," Indigo thought. "I could handle the rattlesnake, and Owl could balk the hawk, but if we tried to, the wild-cat and coyote would get us. Only Gopher and Peba could be proof against physical attack, and they would be in trouble the moment they emerged from their armor. None of us want to tangle with the civet. We are overmatched."

"What about mental?" Rowan asked.

"These are grown animals," Cottontail reminded her. "Their minds are fully developed, and they are experienced. We are not their intellectual equals."

"Maybe not, though I like all of you fine as you are. But what about me?"

"We will take you with us when we go," Gopher thought. "We can still help you conceal your nature, so that you can remain in this realm. But it may be better for you to return to your own realm, for our lives will become much harder without our burrow. It may be long before we are able to lay claim to a new territory, where we can forage in peace, and we won't have resources to trade for the things you need."

"I'll go home if I have to," Rowan thought. "Not for my benefit, because they'll just put me in a boarding school.

But I'd do it for your benefit, because I really—" Her thought broke off, because she was crying again.

"We know you don't want to leave our realm," Cottontail thought. "We don't want you to leave. But neither do we want you to suffer. Would they house you and feed you at the wooden place?"

The girl's tears abruptly became laughter. "Oh, that's a pun! Boarding—board—wood. I didn't know puns were possible with telepathy. Yes, they would take care of me. But I wouldn't have any freedom. I wouldn't be able to be with any of you again, and that—" Her tears were back.

"We will keep you with us as long as you wish," Gopher thought. "But if you do not return now, the other burrow will have possession of the passage to the portal, and you may not be able to do it later. Is this a good risk to take?"

"I don't know," she admitted. "My common sense says I should use the portal while I can. But my heart—my desire—says I should stay here with you. I'm young, like you, and unreformed, so I want to do the foolish thing."

"We understand," Owl thought, and there was a mental murmur of agreement from the others. "We are all young and foolish."

"Then let's stay and fight them," Rowan thought.

"We are not *that* foolish," Indigo thought. "We can't hold this territory against such a group."

"Not physically," she thought. "But I had a notion, back before I got distracted. Maybe we could fight them mentally."

"We do not understand," Gopher thought, thinking for all of them.

"That's good, I think, because it'll work better if the folk here don't understand. Have any of you ever played games? Games of imagination, of pretend?"

"Is this related to deception?" Cottontail asked. "We are not good at that."

"Yes. In my realm we have games—pretend fights— where we try to beat each other without actually hurting anyone. We do it for fun. Like pretend fighting, or role playing."

They gazed blankly at her. This concept was not only new, it seemed indecipherable.

"Like I might pretend to hit Cottontail, but not really do it," Rowan thought, swinging her arm at him but missing. "Just for teasing. For fun."

Cottontail was as blank as the rest of them. "How can it be fun to strike an animal, or to pretend to? I knew you were not going to do it, and if I had not known, I would have been alarmed."

"And if my mind were closed, you could be really alarmed," she thought. She picked Cottontail up and started to heave him at the tree. He tried to jump, alarmed, but before he could do it, her motion slowed. She had not thrown him.

"I do not like that," he thought reprovingly.

She set him down. "And suppose a fire suddenly spread, surrounding you?"

Cottontail looked nervously around. There *was* a fire, racing in a circle around him. There was no avenue clear for him to flee it.

Then it faded. There was no fire. He realized that there had been none; she had merely thought of it in her mind, and her mind was so strong that it had seemed real for a moment. When she was sharing a burrow meeting, her imagination became real for all of them. "I do not like the fire either," he thought.

"Now suppose you're a—a foreign wildcat or something, and you find yourself surrounded by fire, and soon it will burn you. Wouldn't you get out of here as fast as you could?"

"Yes. But there is no fire."

"But there could seem to be, if you burrow folk strengthened my telepathy and I imagined it strongly enough. I could imagine a forest fire, if only I could make others see it."

"We could help you do that," Cottontail agreed. "But to what point? An imaginary fire would not harm anyone."

"To scare away the invading burrow creatures. If enough weird things happened, they might decide to go look somewhere else for their new territory."

Slowly the concept spread through the group of them. What the girl had shown Cottontail was unpleasant. She had done it on her own, because her limited telepathy was effective at close range and they were open to her mind. If the others enhanced it, the effect could be much worse. It could indeed frighten those who did not know it was imaginary.

"But very soon such a fire would be revealed as merely a thought," Owl thought. "An overview would satisfy a creature that it was not dangerous."

"A fire, yes, because it wouldn't actually burn anything. But what about a ghost?"

Again they all were blank.

"Like a dead thing acting alive," Rowan thought. "Let me concentrate again." She frowned, concentrating.

A shadow appeared before Cottontail. It flickered and thickened, assuming the form of a rabbit. An ugly rabbit, with tattered ears and empty spaces for eyes. Suddenly it jumped right at him.

Cottontail fell over backwards, astonished. But the pretend rabbit was gone. "I do not like that either."

"Suppose you kept finding ghost rabbits like that, and maybe nobody else could see them, but they kept jumping at you. Wouldn't you want to get away from them?"

"Yes."

"Even if you were a big tough coyote or something?"

"No one would like this sort of thing," Cottontail thought. "Predators would dislike it as much as anyone."

"So if we could make a slew of bad things to bother them, maybe the members of that other burrow would decide this territory wasn't worth it, and would go away."

This was beginning to make sense. "But we lack experience with this—pretending," Cottontail thought. "We could not fool the other animals more than a moment."

"But suppose you had a really big mind to draw on, that nobody else knew about? One that could imagine a lot of ugly things?"

"This becomes more interesting," Indigo thought. "We do have an associate with such a mind."

"But she is not skilled with telepathy," Peba thought, getting to the bottom of the problem. "She can make such effects only when close by."

"That's why I need your support," Rowan thought. "To enhance me, so I can do it from farther away."

"We would have to be close by you," Owl thought. "That could be awkward, especially if they suspected and looked around for other sapients."

"There is a better way," Peba thought. "But it may be dangerous." He shared his idea.

Rowan clapped her hands together, making a sound, in another of her odd mannerisms. "Double or nothing. That's perfect!"

Maybe it would work. It was not something Cottontail himself would ever have thought of, and it was risky, but it did give them a real chance to prevail. They settled down to work out the details.

Chapter 11
Scare

Peba Armadillo was extremely nervous. He knew the plan, but now he understood the concept of risk, and that was uncomfortable. He had thought of the key aspect, but now almost wished he hadn't. There was so much that could go wrong.

"But if it works, we'll be home free," Rowan thought. She was standing at the base of the tree.

That was true. So Peba curled up in the bottom of her treehouse and oriented his mind on hers, closing out all other contacts. He was here to enhance her telepathy. That, and her closeness to the enemy—(another unusual concept)—were the essence of their plan. He would think through her mind, and she would make monsters like none conceived of before in this realm. It should be terrifying—if the members of the other burrow did not, as Rowan put it, catch on.

But if they did realize what it was, both Rowan and Peba would be in severe trouble. That was the essence of the girl's thought, Double or Nothing. They could win more than otherwise, or lose more than they wanted to.

"They're coming," Rowan thought. "Even with my limited telepathy, I can feel their hostile minds."

"Remember to be humanly stupid," Peba reminded her.

"Duh," she agreed.

The first to arrive was the hawk, flying in to perch on a lower branch of the tree. "What is this?" she demanded arrogantly.

Peba hid his mind. Rowan was supposed to be the only one here. His contact with her was closed to others.

"Me human bearer," Rowan thought.

"Where is the burrow?" The hawk's brusque thought did not mean the hole in the ground, but the burrow mates.

"They go," Rowan thought dully.

"Why didn't you go with them?"

"Me not told to."

The hawk considered. "They left so fast they forgot to take their bearer? That is our fortune. You are now *our* bearer."

"Me do as told," Rowan agreed.

But the hawk was not quite satisfied. "They should have made some protest. Why did they leave so readily?"

"Ghosts."

The hawk had trouble with this concept. "Explain."

"Me not good at explaining." Peba, new to the concept of mirth, nevertheless experienced it. The girl was having fun playing a dummy, fooling the sapient bird.

The hawk become impatient. "Make your best effort."

"Place haunted. Bad things come, scare burrow mates."

"*What* things?"

"This."

Then Rowan imagined a monster from the fantasy of her own realm. It was a vulture with a human face, called a harpy. It flapped in from behind the tree, a huge filthy bird with wild hair and feathers. "Get the hell out of my tree, hawkbill!" the harpy thought, making a raucous screeching noise.

The hawk sailed off her perch, startled in just the way Owl had been when Rowan showed this image to them the first time. It was especially repulsive to a bird, because it was like a gross misshapen bird. A caricature, as Rowan put it.

And the harpy flapped after the hawk. "Come back here, you misbegotten birdbrain! Gimme a kiss!" There was a loud smacking sound as the harpy moved her human lips.

But the hawk had had enough. Peba was able to intercept her thought to her burrow mates as she fled. "This is a bad location. It is haunted. That's why the prior tenants left."

But the next member of the foreign burrow was almost there. This was the coyote, running swiftly. "There are no such things as haunts," she responded. "You're too flighty."

"See for yourself," the hawk thought irately, and continued flying away.

The coyote arrived, and Rowan stood with her staff, assessing him in her terms. She was about one and a half feet high, and twice that long, counting the tail. Big for a sapient, small for a wolf. She could probably bash her off with the pole if she had to.

"Do not do that," Peba thought urgently.

"I won't. I know a bearer would never attack a sapient animal. But if this goes wrong, I'll go down fighting."

The coyote drew up before her, considering this creature. "Who are you?"

"Me bearer. Hawk say me your bearer now."

"Of course, though we hardly need one for travel. You will do brute labor."

"Me brute," Rowan agreed.

"What alarmed Hawk?"

"Ghost."

"I am not familiar with the concept." The coyote did not accept what the hawk had seen.

"Like this."

Rowan conjured her next mental image. It was a wolf, somewhat larger and shaggier than the coyote. "Get away from my tree, bitch!" he thought.

Peba picked up a curiously mixed reaction from Rowan. She had thought a term that could be used as either a female wolf or a bad word. She had used it both ways at once. She liked doing that, being unreformed.

The coyote backed away. "I did not feel you coming. What are you?"

"A werewolf." And the wolf shifted into a brutish human man. "Get out, or tangle with me, you bad excuse for a dog!" The man grabbed for the coyote.

The coyote danced out of the way. "This is not possible. Animals do not exchange shapes."

"It is possible for a werewolf." The wolf form reappeared. "Now I'll take a piece of you." He snapped at the coyote, his huge jaws slavering. Peba helped boost the enormous surge of menace that accompanied the snap.

The coyote's nerve broke. She fled, with the werewolf bounding after her, growling.

"What do you think of haunts now?" the hawk's thought came from a distance.

"Something very strange here," the coyote replied. "I don't think that werewolf was real, but I don't want its company."

"You both are timid," the wildcat thought as she bounded past the retreating coyote. "I shall see what in going on."

"Me dull bearer," Rowan thought as the wildcat came to the tree. "Me left behind."

"Think when thought to," the wildcat responded curtly. She sniffed around the entrance to the burrow, then considered the tree. "What is this structure in the tree?"

"Me house," the dull human responded. "Me not fit in burrow."

"This burrow went to a lot of trouble for you."

"Me good bearer."

"I see no haunts."

Then a panther sprang from behind the tree. He was twice the wildcat's size. "Get away from my tree, tabby cat!" he thought fiercely.

The wildcat was taken aback, but not intimidated. She was a scarred veteran of many violent encounters; Peba read that in her mind. "Where did you come from?"

"I am the ghost of this tree. I chomp anyone who molests it. Now get out of here before I chomp you." The panther advanced on the wildcat, radiating menace.

"There are no panthers in this region," the wildcat thought. "You can't be real." Then she sprang at the panther—and right through him, for indeed, he wasn't real.

This was mischief. The panther had caught on, and would let the others know.

But Rowan was a quick thinker. "I am a ghost," the panther agreed. "But I can still hurt you."

"How, when you can't touch me?"

"By taking over the body of the human," the panther thought. "I am not physical, but she is."

"A stupid human?" the wildcat thought derisively.

The panther leaped at Rowan, and merged with her body. Then she thought with its tone of mind, which was of course easy for her to do, since she had been imagining it all along. "Now I have a body. It may be clumsy, but it will do."

"This is not possible," the wildcat thought, but there was doubt in her mind. No human of this realm had ever thought in such a manner.

The possessed human lifted the staff and stepped menacingly toward the wildcat. "Now I will smash you, kitty cat!" Rowan thought, striking with the pole.

The wildcat readily avoided the blow, but her confidence was shaken. The panther did seem to have become physical, in its fashion, and it was remarkably aggressive.

"Bearer!" the wildcat thought urgently. "Retreat!"

"I have possession of this body, not you, you mangy feline," the ghost thought. "You can't order *me* around!" And the body made a lunge with the pole.

The wildcat's nerve broke. She turned tail and fled.

Rowan leaned against the tree, keeping a tight rein on her mind. Peba know why: she had been bluffing, and now was weak with reaction. The point had not been to beat back the wildcat, though she might have done it with the staff, but to convince it that something supernatural was happening. That had finally worked, in part because no human bearer would have attacked a sapient animal. But if the wildcat had not been bluffed, the whole case could have been lost.

"Banish the panther," Peba thought. "The civet is arriving, and it is canny."

"No, maybe it is better to set it back with my mind,"

Rowan thought. "As the ghost, showing another power: it can make a dull human smart."

"But if she realizes that it is your real mind—"

"She shouldn't. There is no mind like mine in this realm, so it must be a ghost. I hope."

Peba hoped so too. The members of the other burrow were increasingly difficult to scare off, and all of them had to be scared, or all was lost.

The civet cat arrived. She was black with white stripes patterning her small body, and the end of her tail was bushy white.

"That's no cat!" Rowan thought, alarmed. "That's a skunk!"

"Yes, a variety of skunk," Peba agreed. "Didn't you know?"

"Where I come from they aren't called cats."

"But Owl sent a mental picture."

"I guess I picked up on the name, and never actually looked at the picture. That's a lesson for me: look before I assume. Now I know why none of you want to tangle with a civet. I don't want to tangle with her either. She could raise an awful stink."

Meanwhile the skunk was surveying the situation. She was a handsome creature, and she did not smell bad. "A panther taking over the body of a human bearer?" she thought, picking up on what her burrow mate had thought. "I doubt it. Something else is going on here."

Peba felt the girl's nervousness about dealing with such a creature, and her determination to play it through. There was no ready alternative. "Not a panther, a ghost. I assume any form I choose, or I take over any body I choose. Maybe I'll take yours." She stepped toward the skunk. It was sheer bluff.

The skunk was dubious, but careful. She retreated, not turning tail either to flee or to spray her awful stink. "You could be a rogue human pretending to be possessed by a ghost."

"Does any human have a mind like this?" Rowan opened her mind, with a blast of sheer power. It was similar to the experience of Peba and the others when they first shared minds with her, but this was a hostile presentation.

The skunk tried to doubt, but could not, because this was real. The human mind really was impossibly powerful. About to be swept away by its tempestuous strength, the skunk turned and ran away, not even trying to spray.

"Halt!" Rowan thought after her. "I want to eat your mind!"

But the skunk had had more than enough. She was getting as far away as possible.

Peba and Rowan relaxed again, both feeling weak from the encounter. Had the skunk not been successfully bluffed, Rowan could have gotten sprayed, and both she and the tree would have smelled awful for a long time. This scare-project was not turning out to be easy.

The fifth member of the invading burrow arrived. This was the rattlesnake. She was full grown, thick of body and cynical of mind. "There have been some odd things here," she thought. "But I think nothing that a good shot of venom can't cure."

"Do not let her get within striking range!" Peba thought urgently. "If she coils, get away!"

Rowan held her staff firmly before her, ready to block the snake. She was afraid of rattlesnakes; her fear made her body feel weak. Peba sent reassurance, though he feared for her too. "Yes, very odd," Rowan thought to the rattlesnake.

"What would a bearer know of it?"

"Remember to be stupid," Peba thought warningly.

Roman checked herself; she had been about to forget. "Only what me see."

The snake remained wary. "What do you see?"

"A dragon." And around the tree came a huge serpentine creature with a ferocious head gleaming with teeth.

This did set the rattlesnake back. "What manner of snake are you?"

"A ghost snake," he replied. "I breathe fire."

"Impossible. No snake associates with fire."

The dragon inhaled enormously, then blew out a fierce

column of fire that missed to the side. That was deliberate, because the fire was illusionary; if it struck the rattlesnake, there would be no heat, and the bluff would be
exposed.

The rattlesnake wriggled like a sidewinder, sideways,
away from the flame. "This can't be!"

"You have much to learn about ghosts," the dragon
thought. "Now are you going to leave my tree alone, or will
I have to scorch your tail?"

"A ghost, as you think it, has no substance," the rattlesnake thought.

"So you can't bite me. But I can scorch you." The
dragon inhaled again, orienting his snout directly on the
rattlesnake.

The rattlesnake fled. She disappeared into the brush,
but they were able to follow her mind. She had not realized that Rowan's logic was not valid; if the ghost could
not be touched, neither could it touch or burn. Another
bluff had been successful.

But there was one more to go. This was the tortoise,
the slowest member of the group, but also the least likely
one to spook. A ghost would probably not scare her.

"We'll have to think of something else," Rowan
thought. "What would keep a tortoise out of a burrow?

"A flood," Peba thought. "The same thing that would
keep out other animals."

"But this burrow is too well drained. That tunnel to
the portal goes really deep, but there was never any water.
She'd just go down in it, and soon know the water wasn't
real."

"Yes, tortoises are practical," Peba agreed. "As long
as they have room to fit, and air to breathe, they are satisfied."

"Air," she thought. "How about bad air?"

"The air here is good."

"But it could seem bad in the burrow. Like poison
gas. Suffocating. She wouldn't like that."

"But if she can still breathe—"

"Like this." She concentrated.

The air around Peba became close, and it smelled

bad. He tried to take a breath, but it felt like bitter water. "I'm drowning!"

The air freshened immediately. "You only felt as if you were drowning," she thought. "And you know it's not real. Would it work on a tortoise who didn't know?"

"Yes!" Peba gasped. He had not liked the bad air at all.

"I'll tell her it's bad, and maybe she won't believe me, but when she goes into the burrow I'll make it feel like that, and she'll have enough belief to be scared."

"This is more likely to work than a ghost panther or dragon," Peba agreed. "Down under ground, it is easier to believe in bad air."

"That's what I figure."

They waited, and in due course the tortoise arrived. She was larger than Gopher, with a heavier shell, and her mind was far more experienced. She was tougher than any of the predators. She had been mistress of her burrow for many years, and knew the secrets of a number of animals. She did not believe in harpies, dragons, werewolves, ghosts, or possession. She intended to take over this burrow, and that was all there was to it. Her burrow mates would be less timid when they saw that she had occupied it.

"Hello, Tortoise," Rowan thought as the female came near the tree.

The tortoise ignored her. Uppity bearers could be retrained as convenient. She headed directly for the burrow entrance.

"Air there bad," Rowan thought, emulating stupid. "Poison. Choke. Die."

The tortoise did not deign to respond. She entered the burrow and headed down into its depths.

Rowan imagined a faint bad odor, as of a distant whiff of dead animal. She increased this to a worse odor, as of a nearby rotting carcass. Then she imagined mustard gas filling the burrow, making anything within it choke and gasp for breath. It was rising from below, from the region of the portal, a sickly stench. It intensified into nausea, becoming almost liquid. It was impossible to survive in this putrid fog. Any creature who remained here long would suffocate. In fact the tunnel was starting to spin around dizzyingly, suggesting a mind that was fading. What an awful way to die!

The tortoise emerged from the burrow. She moved rapidly (for a tortoise) away. Her mind was revolted; that was the worst smelling burrow she had encountered.

Peba shared a joyful feeling with Rowan. They had bluffed out the last invader.

Soon the burrow mates returned, having tuned in on the proceedings from a distance. They were quite pleased. Rowan had done it; she had driven away the enemy burrow.

After that they relaxed. Peba was quite worn, emotionally, and preferred to remain right where he was, curled up in the treehouse, while Rowan worked to perfect her roof and the details of the interior. She used extra sections of cloth to bind dry grass and make pillows she could rest against, because her body lacked the bony surface an armadillo had. Then she used the howdah to take Cottontail to the grazing field. Peba went too, and dug for bugs, finding some good ones. Owl, Indigo, and Gopher slept in the burrow. It was a wonderful, easygoing time.

But next morning that changed. This time Cottontail, who had spent the night on one of Rowan's soft pillows, was the first to tune in to the threat. "The female burrow is coming back!" he thought to everyone.

They all came awake. How could this happen? They had driven off every member of that hostile burrow. The predators should be looking far away for their new residence.

Owl did a flyby, tuning in, and got the answer: they had had a burrow meeting, compared notes, considered, and caught on that they had been fooled. So they were coming again, this time all together. They would arrive before noon. It was, as Rowan thought of it, crisis time.

Meanwhile, the home burrow had its own meeting. "They know they were fooled," Owl reported. "But they don't know exactly *how* they were fooled. They want to find out, so they can't be stopped like that again. They are predators; they don't like feeling like victims."

"Neither do we," Cottontail thought. Every twinge of
his leg reminded him of his status as victim.

"So have we lost after all?" Gopher asked.

"We can't stand against them now, any better than we
could before," Peba thought. "Our only hope lay in deceiving them. We will not be able to do that again."

"I'm not so sure," Rowan thought. "The easiest person to fool is the one who thinks he knows all the an-
swers. Maybe we just have to find a better way to fool
them."

The others were blank; they did not know of another
way. Peba struggled to think of one, but could not. "We
lack your power of mind," he thought. "You must think of
it, if you can."

"Well, let's see," Rowan thought. "They know we're
doing something, but they don't realize that it's coming
from my mind. Maybe that will be enough."

Peba still didn't see how. "They know that what scared
them off before were illusions. They must want to find the
source of those illusions. The moment you do something,
they'll know."

"Not necessarily. I'm a dumb human, remember; no
one ever heard of imagination in one of those, let alone
sapience. I read this story once, about weird things happening, and it turned out to be a big tree doing it. It took
forever for them to figure that out, because no one believed a tree could have a mind. Just as the folk of this
realm don't believe a human could have a mind. Why don't
we pretend it's the tree doing it, maybe because it likes
us, and will haunt them forever if they stay near it?"

That began to make sense. Rowan had her tree house;
the tree might tolerate her because it liked her and the
burrow. Maybe they protected it from bugs that wanted to
bore into its bark. If they told the other burrow it was the
tree, then the others would know that they couldn't get
rid of it, because the tree could not be moved.

"But we must not tell them that," Rowan cautioned.

Peba was surprised. "But this is what we want them
to believe. We must tell them."

"No. We must try not to tell them. Then they will be-lieve."

The others looked at her. Why was she thinking such obvious nonsense?"

"Boys, you'll have to trust me on this one. I've been fooled often, and learned how it's done. This is the way to do it."

"We find this hard to believe," Gopher thought.

"I'll explain." She did, and slowly it made sense. None of them would ever have thought of it themselves, but they had not had Rowan's experience with deception. They did have to trust her.

They worked out the details, as they had before, and were ready for the other burrow. Peba was not at all sure this would work, for the human reasoning was contrary to common sense, but he was ready to play his part. They all were, for the future of their burrow depended on it.

This time the predator burrow arrived in style, using their own bearer for their tortoise. It was a big human man with a supremely dull look on his face, using a how-dah. The hawk perched on his shoulder, and the coyote, wildcat, skunk, and rattlesnake kept pace with him.

The assembled mates of the local burrow stood around the tree, awaiting the visitors. This would be a double burrow meeting, to forge an agreement. They had no choice; to flee would be to yield their territory. But it seemed likely that they would have to yield it anyway.

The bearer sat on the ground, but the tortoise did not dismount. The others settled around the bearer. They were a formidable looking group, and knew it; they gazed at the members of the other burrow with hardly-veiled contempt. "We know you fooled us," the tortoise thought. "Now we shall discover how."

"We do not care to inform you," Gopher replied. But there was some hesitancy in his mind; he was evidently daunted by the immediate presence of the predator group. The coyote and wildcat were looking at Cottontail and lick-ing their chops. This was a formal meeting; no hunting was allowed. But they seemed to be on the verge of violat-ing the truce. It was a deliberate show, but effective.

Peba, now on the ground beside the tree, let slip a nervous thought. "It's the tree."

"Close your mind!" Gopher snapped, too late.

"What is this about the tree?" the tortoise demanded.

"Our burrow is by a tree," Gopher thought. "Our bearer lives in the tree. That is all."

"That is not all. You juveniles are not good at masking your thoughts." The tortoise gazed sternly at Peba. "What were you thinking?"

"Nothing," Peba thought, frightened; he did not have to pretend about that. "It is just a tree."

But at this point Cottontail, quite nervous about the nearness of so many formidable predators, was unable to suppress a thought. "It's a ghost tree."

"Ghosts," the tortoise thought. "Things that appear but do not exist."

"No, the tree is solid," Gopher thought quickly.

"I would not credit this notion," the tortoise thought. "But we did see ghosts, and they were in the vicinity of this tree. But how can a tree make such images?"

"It can't," Gopher thought. "It is just an ordinary tree."

But Owl, nervous under the steady gaze of the hawk, could not quite suppress a thought. "It's a most unusual tree. We were amazed."

"All of the ghosts were near this tree," the tortoise repeated. "Several came from behind the tree, yet there is nothing there. It could be the tree."

Peba kept his real thought thoroughly hidden. The predators were doing it—fooling themselves. Just as Rowan had thought they would. Her experience in deception was proving out. It was amazing.

Suddenly the coyote, wildcat, and rattlesnake focused their thoughts on Indigo, who was relaxed, not guarding his mind tightly. It was obviously a rehearsed mental pounce, with considerable power, and it worked. Indigo's topmost thoughts were abruptly laid bare. "The tree likes us. It protects us. It scares intruders away." Then, appalled, Indigo closed his mind.

"Yet a tree can have no mind of its own," the tortoise thought. "A tree is not sapient. Who directs it to do this?"

"No one," Gopher thought. But his thought lacked force.

"Let us make this straightforward," the tortoise thought. Peba noticed that none of the predators had their minds open; they were leaving it all to their landlord. That was impressive discipline. "We have seen the ghosts. How much can this tree do?"

Gopher's resistance collapsed. His burrow was defeated, and he obviously knew it. "Anything we can imagine. We have gotten good at imagination."

"Make a fire."

Gopher sent a hopeless thought to the others, ignoring Rowan. "Join with me. Signal the tree. Make a fire."

And it was Rowan who unleashed her imagination, masked by the efforts of the burrow mates surrounding her. A ball of fire appeared before the tree. It dropped to the ground, igniting the dry leaves and grass. It spread rapidly, a line of it sweeping toward the predators.

But this time the predators were not spooked. They held their places as the fire approached, and as it passed through them without burning. It was seeming fire, without heat. It moved on, making the trees flare up, sending clouds of smoke into the sky.

The tortoise sent a thought to the predators. "Douse the fire."

They tried, but their massed thoughts had no effect. The fire spread through the forest, making torches of the trees. It was unstoppable.

The tortoise addressed Gopher. "Douse the fire."

"Douse the fire," Gopher repeated to the burrow mates. They focused their thoughts—and the fire faded away.

"Make a flood," the tortoise thought.

Gopher directed the burrow mates, and they imagined a flood. Water surged out of the burrow, washing across the ground, inundating the animals of both groups. All of them stayed put; the water had no substance. But it seemed real.

"Dry the flood," the female tortoise thought to the predators. They tried, but again their thoughts had no effect.

"The tree obeys only us," Gopher explained. "Because it knows us and likes us."

"In time it would come to know us."

"It remains attuned to us. We will not let you rest, if you take our burrow and territory."

Then a swarm of biting flies appeared. They zoomed in on the predators, stinging them. The stings were not real, but several predators flinched, not liking this.

"We will make your lives miserable," Gopher thought. "You may displace us from our territory, but we can reach this tree mentally from far away."

The dragon appeared. It shot a jet of fire at the predators. They flinched again; the fire seemed too real.

"We will keep doing this," Gopher thought. "Because we hate losing our burrow."

The tortoise considered. Then its bearer stood and walked away from the tree. The predators accompanied it.

The other burrow had given up. Thanks to Rowan's deceptive strategy.

Chapter 12
Burrow

Indigo had caught a fine rat, and was ready to settle for a week in the burrow to digest it, when a howdah approached. It was mounted on a grown human female, and carried an Elder Tortoise. This was unusual, for elders seldom traveled.

The other burrow mates were out foraging; Indigo was the only one near the burrow, guarding it until someone else came back. They always kept at least one mate near the burrow, because that established their occupancy. So Indigo remained by the entrance, awaiting the tortoise. This was obviously important business.

The human stopped. The tortoise gazed down from the platform. "Identity?" His mind was peremptory and powerful; he was definitely a creature of authority. Certainly in matters relating to tortoises, and to burrows, and thus Indigo himself, because he was a burrow mate. The Council of Tortoises was supreme in burrow matters.

"Indigo Snake, of this burrow." He did not volunteer further thought; Elders of any species preferred to control dialogue.

"There has been a complaint made against this group."

Indigo could not restrain himself. "A complaint! How can that be? We have done nothing evil."

"The complaint is that a rogue band of squatters are

occupying this territory, and using an alien animal to re-pel a legitimate burrow that wishes to take possession."

"A rogue band! We are a forming burrow, lacking only our sixth burrow mate before we petition for recognition."

"Precisely. You are not a formal burrow, so have no rights to this territory. You must give way to any recog-nized burrow that wishes to establish itself here. Such a burrow has petitioned the Council for justice, and cus-tom requires that this be granted in three days if there is no refutation of the case."

Three days! This felt like doom. "And what is this about an alien animal?" But beneath his thought, Indigo had a sick suspicion what was meant.

"A juvenile human female with a frighteningly unstable mind. Any human who thinks aggressively at sapients is dangerous, and must be abolished. Its very presence would suffice to make your petition ineligible, even if you had a sixth mate."

This was disaster! Obviously the enemy burrow had caught on to Rowan's role, and was now striking against her. If she had to go, their burrow would have no defense against the predator burrow, and would lose its territory.

Indigo feared they were lost, just when they thought they had won. Evidently the others had not been fooled by the story of the tree, and had fathomed the true source of the illusions. Unable to get rid of Rowan directly, they were doing it legally. They would win, unless the home burrow came up with something outstanding.

What could they do? Indigo wished the others were here, to enhance their thinking together. But he was alone, with only his limited mind. How could he slither into a winning strategy?

He did something desperate: he groveled. "We mean no harm, Elder. We did not know we were in violation of a rule. We are just trying to become a burrow, and are al-most there. The human girl was in trouble in her own realm, so we took her in as our bearer; she is no monster. She was just trying to help us. Please, Elder Tortoise: tell us our best course."

The tortoise considered, and for a moment Indigo

thought he would not deign to answer. But then he did. "We are aware of your innocence in this matter, and understand that the human is not a real threat to the existing order. We are obliged to follow established custom. A recognized burrow has precedence over an incomplete one, but normally does not seek to displace those who have developed a territory. Your best course is to send the alien human away, get a legitimate sixth mate, and petition for recognition as an established burrow. If you can accomplish this within three days, you will have tenure, and that will enable you to prevail."

"Thank you, Elder! We will try."

But the bearer was already walking away in response to the elder's directive. Indigo had the impression that the tortoise had given more advice than was necessary, but did not want this known. Maybe it would damage the impartiality for which the Council of Tortoises was known.

That evening they held a burrow meeting. Indigo shared the news of the legal challenge to their burrow, and the advice the elder had given. "So he has shown us a way, if we can manage it," he concluded. "But it is not a way I like."

"So they weren't fooled," Rowan thought, dejected. "You know, I thought I smelled skunk, but of course that was possible, since the skunk was there. But she never thought anything; she was silent. Now I think she was into my mind, while I was distracted making the illusions. We thought we were fooling them, but they were fooling us, distracting us while the skunk quietly read my mind."

"It did seem rather easy," Gopher agreed. "They challenged us, and then went away."

"So we were suckered," Rowan thought. "And instead of helping you, I hurt you, because my presence makes you ineligible to be a burrow. I'm really sorry about that. But I can fix it; I'll go back to my realm, so you can get your sixth burrow mate and hold your territory."

But Indigo felt her grief; she did not want to go. And they did not want her to go; they all liked her. "We must find another way," he thought, and felt the general agreement.

"Yet the Elder told us to send her away," Gopher thought. "And to get a sixth burrow mate. In only three days."

"If we can get a sixth mate," Peba thought. "How can we do in three days what we haven't done in six months?"

"Even then, it isn't certain," Owl thought glumly. "Why let her go, when we might lose the territory anyway? I'd rather keep her and look for new territory."

"No, I have to go," Rowan thought. "I never meant to interfere with your burrow. You've done so much for me, it just isn't fair to cost you everything."

A strange idea was wriggling through Indigo's mind. Finally he caught it. "We have two problems. First, to keep Rowan. Second to get a sixth burrow mate. Can we combine them?"

"What are you thinking!" Rowan thought, astonished.

"They are mutually exclusive, unfortunately," Cottontail thought. "Either the presence of the girl, or the lack of a mate, is enough to make us ineligible."

"But *are* they?" Indigo asked. "If we can qualify her as sapient and not dangerous, she might be acceptable. We know we want her; this would enable us to keep her. We must address this question: can she be made acceptable?"

They considered that. "I'll stay out of this," Rowan thought tearfully. "But I thank you for even considering it."

"No human has ever been a burrow mate, anywhere," Gopher thought.

"No human has ever been sapient, in this realm," Indigo replied. "Now one is."

"But the Council of Tortoises would not accept a human," Owl thought.

"They might reconsider, if they encountered a sapient one," Indigo replied.

Gopher remained dubious. "We have very little time. We might qualify, if we follow the Elder's advice. We probably won't, if we don't."

"It is a gamble," Peba agreed, drawing on one of the new concepts they had acquired from Rowan.

It was Cottontail who leaped to the conclusion they liked. "If we send her away, and get another mate, and are approved, we will never be really satisfied, for we'll never forget her. If we try to qualify Rowan, and fail, we won't be a recognized burrow, and we'll lose our territory, but we will still be together. I would rather lose that way than win the other way."

There was a pause. Then their minds coalesced. "Losing is winning," Indigo thought. "We want Rowan more than we want our territory."

"And we just might win," Owl thought.

"We will do it," Gopher thought, for all of them.

"Oh thank you!" Rowan thought. "I could just hug and kiss you all!"

"Do not do that," Owl thought hastily.

Rowan laughed, and they shared her mirth. It was another of her concepts they were learning and liking.

"Now we must be practical," Peba thought. "Rowan will not qualify if she is seen as stupid. Neither will she succeed if she is seen as smarter than normal sapient animals. Or if she seems dangerously imaginative. The Council will be wary of her because of the predator burrow's complaint. We must show them that she is sapient and safe."

"This is difficult," Rowan thought. "Because I'm *not* safe. It would be really bad if any more like me got into this realm."

"It would," Gopher agreed.

"But I'm not sure your plan will work," Rowan thought. "Because you want to satisfy the tortoises that I'm not smarter than other sapient animals. But I *am* smarter. I don't want to lie about it, not to the Council, and I don't think I could fool them anyway. They should accept or reject me as I am."

They considered that. None of them had been good at deception, and they now knew that their efforts had not worked before.

"But if you show your true mind to the Council, they will know, and the other animals will not like it," Peba thought.

"Well, the raccoons know, and they aren't wary," Rowan thought. "Maybe the Elder Tortoises will be satisfied to keep the secret too."

"I think they would," Gopher agreed. "They don't specialize in secrets, but they need to know things in order to treat burrow matters fairly."

"They said they knew we were innocent, and that Rowan was not a threat," Indigo reminded them. "So they may know more than they indicated."

"And they would not like it if we tried to deceive them," Cottontail thought, leaping to another conclusion. "They may judge our case by the honesty with which we present it."

The others considered that, and agreed.

"We shall prepare our case for the first human burrow mate," Gopher thought.

"And present it in two days," Indigo thought. "So that if it is accepted, we are there first, and we have tenure, and can keep our territory."

After that, they scattered for the early evening hunting and foraging, all of them thinking about the matter. Rowan was pondering it too, as she harvested more vegetables from the fox's garden. They all knew that they had no certainty of success. The Council could decide either way, and probably against them. They had to make the best possible case, and hope that it was accepted.

Indigo, curling in his chamber to digest his meal, was uneasy. The predator burrow had shown itself to be smart and determined. It might not leave the matter up to the Council of Tortoises. It would of course argue against allowing a human to become a burrow mate. But would it leave it at that? What ugly surprise could it have, to make its victory certain? Indigo didn't know, but he planned to be alert.

In the morning they organized and set off. Rowan wore the bearer garb, and the howdah. Gopher and Cottontail rode the platform, not too big a weight for the girl to handle. Indigo and Owl traveled on their own. Peba remained at the burrow, to maintain possession, just in case a member of the predator burrow tried to move in during their absence.

They were traveling to the nearest Council station, one day's journey away. The Council of Tortoises governed burrow matters across the continent, but did not meet physically. Instead they met mentally, knowing each other well enough to establish a long distance network. So there would be only one Elder Tortoise there, but the full Council would decide.

Indigo was most familiar with the region near the council station, so led the way. He knew where the dangers were, and routed around them, while Owl flew in great circles above, checking for anything that might be a problem.

"Beware," Owl thought. "There's a panther in the area."

Indigo looped back and relayed the news to the howdah party. A panther was too big a predator to ignore; they would need to be ready to mind-stun it if it got an idea about going after the human girl. Normally the big cats left humans alone, because they worked for sapient animals, but this wasn't always the case.

"What is it hunting?" Rowan asked.

Owl checked. "A bear cub. It has the cub treed, and is making sure the mother bear isn't near before it climbs the tree to get the cub."

"A bear cub," Rowan thought. "I know two cubs, from when I stayed in the bears' cave. Could this be one of them?"

"It is the bears' territory," Owl thought. "It could be. Other bears would be unlikely to intrude."

"Then we'd better check, because those cubs are my friends and I don't want them killed."

Indigo suppressed his annoyance at this delay. The girl was loyal to the cubs, as she was to the burrow. He couldn't fault her for loyalty. They detoured to locate the cub.

Meanwhile Owl flew down to perch on a branch of the cub's tree. "Who are you?" he thought.

The cub was terrified. It was soon clear that he was one of the ones Rowan knew. He had gone exploring on his own while his mother and sister slept, and the panther had winded him and realized he was alone. He had made it up the tree, but now could not get home, and knew that the panther would soon come up after him.

Owl relayed the information to the others. Soon the howdah party would arrive. "Depart," Indigo thought to the panther. "This prey is not for you."

"This is none of your business, snake," the panther thought.

"We made an alliance with the bears," Indigo thought. "We choose to protect this cub."

"I will bite you in half!" It was no bluff; the panther pounced on Indigo.

But of course Indigo slithered out of the way too fast to be caught. Then he linked minds with the burrow mates, and sent a mind hammer strike back at the cat.

The panther tumbled, losing control of its legs. Then it righted itself, but it had acquired respect. It had not realized that the rest of the burrow was close enough to strike in that manner. "Have it your way," it thought, and slunk away.

"Watch the cat," Indigo thought to Owl. "This may be a ruse to get the cub out of the tree and vulnerable."

"You watch the cat," Owl thought. "I will fly to the cave to notify the bears."

Indigo tuned into the panther's mind. Sure enough, it was lurking nearby, awaiting its opportunity.

"I'll carry him home," Rowan thought. She approached the tree. "Cub, I know you," she thought to him. "I visited your cave, and spent a night with your mother and sister."

The cub recognized her. "Nice human!" She lifted up her arms, and took him carefully down from the tree. Then she carried him toward the cave.

They were met part way there by the mother bear. "You saved my cub!" she thought.

"We're friends," Rowan reminded her. "I couldn't let the panther eat him." She set the cub down, and he ran to join his mother.

The panther gave up the hunt in disgust. It could not

get the cub when the mother was with him. A panther was formidable, but a grown bear was more than a match for it.

"But you owed us nothing," the mother bear thought, perplexed.

"I just had to do it," Rowan thought. "Now we must go to meet the Council of Tortoises."

The mother bear struggled with a concept that was somewhat beyond her level, for she was not fully sapient. "Grateful."

"It's okay," Rowan thought. "Maybe some day a panther will have *me* up a tree, and if you're in the neighborhood, you can help me."

"Help you," the bear agreed. Then she and the cub departed. Indigo was amazed at how well the girl had communicated with the bear; she must have lent some of her sapience to it, so that it responded more intelligently than otherwise. She had a certain talent that way; all of them were smarter in her presence than otherwise.

They resumed their journey. But now they were late, and this was going to bring mischief. Indigo couldn't blame Rowan for saving the cub, but it might turn out to be a very expensive gesture.

There was one large river to cross. Because they were now on a main trail, there was a shallow section where animals and their bearers could wade across during the middle of the day. There were alligators, but they were not allowed to molest any creature in the crossing bar at that time. If any did, there would be a mass-mind alligator hunt that would rid the river of the offender. Alligators, like bears, were only half sapient, but they understood the rule and punishment well enough. Safe crossing was honored.

But they reached the river late. It was afternoon, and the alligators had full range. They would have to wait until tomorrow to make the crossing.

"But that will use up our margin," Rowan protested. "We want to get there early."

It was true. But none of them could cross when the alligators were hunting. They would be bitten, drowned, and eaten.

"I wish I'd realized," Rowan thought. "But I still wouldn't have let that panther eat that bear cub."

Indigo understood that, because he was in touch with her mind. Her sense of community went beyond the burrow.

They prepared to camp beside the river, as there was nothing else to do. Then a big male bear approached. Too big; if he attacked, they would have to use the mind hammer, because none of them could oppose him physically.

Indigo slithered out to meet him. "We are traveling, seeking no quarrel," he thought.

"Cross river," the bear thought.

"We will cross the river, but must wait until tomorrow."

"Cross river now."

What was bothering this bear? "Alligators," Indigo explained. "Not safe."

Rowan's thought joined them. "Didn't I see you at the bear cave?" she asked the bear.

"Cave," the bear agreed. "Cubs."

Indigo felt her sudden delight. "You are one of the cave bears! You came to help us, because we saved your cub."

"Saved cub," the bear agreed. He understood her better than he could communicate.

"And now you will do us a favor in return. Like helping us cross the river."

"Cross river," the bear agreed.

Indigo was amazed. The bears had grasped enough of the principle to honor it. This bear must have followed them, looking for a chance to help, and here it was.

They braved the river. Indigo led the way again, swimming. Owl flew watchfully above. Rowan carried Gopher and Cottontail on the howdah. She waded into the river, following Indigo. Soon she was waist deep.

"Alligator!" Owl thought, spotting it from above.

"Where?" Indigo asked. "Tell the bear!"

Owl sent a location picture to the bear. The alligator was swimming right for Rowan.

The bear charged into the water, making a great splash. He lifted up his forelegs, becoming tall. He pointed his snout at the alligator. "Go!" he roared mentally and sonically.

The alligator hesitated. This was more than it had counted on. Then it swerved and went for Indigo.

But Owl tracked it, and the bear charged forward. He brushed close by Rowan, causing her to stumble. Then he lunged for the alligator, snapping his jaws.

The alligator swerved aside again, avoiding the bear. It circled, seeing whether it could still get at the others.

The bear stood again. He made a hugging motion with his great front legs, his formidable claws showing. His eye and mind were locked on the alligator.

It was becoming clear: if there was one creature who could balk an alligator in shallow water, it was a big bear. This bear was doing it. Maybe it would be a different story in deep water—and maybe not. The bear had muscles and teeth and claws, and he was twice as massive as the alligator. He might not be able to catch the alligator if it was just the two of them, but he could intercept it if it came for Indigo or Rowan. Once he got hold of it, he would do some real harm. "Go!" he roared again.

Reluctantly, the alligator retreated. Indigo resumed swimming, and Rowan resumed wading. The bear followed closely after them.

Another alligator came. Owl targeted it, putting its location in the bear's mind, and the bear growled. The alligator kept its distance.

They made it safely to the far shore. "Thank you, Bear," Rowan thought as she stood on the bank. "We are even."

"Even," the bear agreed. Then he turned around and swam back across the river. Neither alligator bothered him.

They resumed their trek. They were still late, but not nearly as late as they would have been. Indigo mulled over what had happened. Burrow mates helped each other, and bears helped other bears of their cave, and sometimes the two made deals, as they had when Rowan spent the night in the bear cave. But a spaced exchange of favors was normally beyond the comprehension of bears. Rowan had done it, by enhancing the bears' understanding. This was an aspect of her mind that the burrow mates had not understood before.

When dusk came, they camped for the night. Rowan had vegetables in her pack, and Indigo didn't need to eat, as he was still digesting his rat. So Indigo guarded Gopher and Cottontail as they grazed, while Owl hunted mice.

Rowan climbed into a branching tree for the night, with Cottontail in her pack. Owl perched on a branch, and Gopher and Indigo rested by the trunk. It wasn't comfortable being away from the burrow, but they managed.

In the morning they resumed travel. They reached the burrow of the Council Tortoise at midday. The mates of the predator burrow were already there, with their human bearer, hoping that they would be the only ones. Had Gopher's burrow not made it within three days, it would have lost the case by default.

The Elder Tortoise was on his bearer's howdah. In deference, the others were on the ground. The predator's human male sat to the side, uninterested in the proceedings, sinking into a snooze. But Rowan sat close, facing the Elder.

Gopher made the case. "We wish to make this human girl our sixth burrow mate," he thought. "She is sapient."

"She is a dangerous rogue human," the predator tortoise thought. "She must be banished."

The Elder's mind focused on Rowan, and Indigo felt its power, augmented by that of the linked Council members. "Open your mind."

Rowan opened her mind to the tortoises. This time Indigo was on the edge, not fully sharing the experience, but he knew what it was: a phenomenal expansion of intellect, awesome in its reach and detail. Indigo felt the Elders' amazement. The girl was not just sapient, she was superior. There was no other mind like hers in this realm.

And if that scared off the Elder Tortoises, their plea was doomed.

"The bears," the Elder thought. "What was that inter-action?"

Now Gopher reviewed what had happened. "She knew the cub. She acted to save it. So the bears helped us cross the river."

"This resembles a burrow interaction," the Elder thought. "But it was beyond the burrow, with non-sapient animals."

"She has that effect," Gopher agreed. "It is one reason we want her. She will make us better."

The predator tortoise protested. "She makes ghosts with her mind. She is dangerous. We must not have a mere human among us with power like that."

The Elder oriented on Rowan again. "Make a ghost."

Rowan made the image of a fire. It started on the ground before her, then rapidly spread outward, passing through the animals and reaching the trees. The Elders were impressed, but not favorably.

"This human is sapient and well meaning," the Elder thought. "But also dangerous. It may not be good to have her in this realm, or as a burrow mate. We are unable to make a decision."

Indigo hated that. No decision was a negative decision, because their burrow was incomplete without its sixth member. Rowan had to be approved, or they were lost.

"May I speak?" Rowan thought.

The Elder hesitated. This was an irregular request. But then the curiosity of the Elders prevailed. They wanted to know more about this strange human. "Yes."

"You're right. I am sapient, and I am dangerous to this realm. If you banish me, I will go back to my own realm. But I don't think you should do that, because though I am the only human of my kind here, I am one of millions there. Any of those humans would be dangerous here, and I don't want them to come here any more than you do. But they might come. There may be other portals we don't know about, and the humans will come, and it will be terrible. But if you let me stay, I will do all that I can to stop any others like me from coming here. That will make you safer. I know what my kind is like, and I might be able to stop others from coming, if I have the support of my burrow. Because I am learning telepathy, and the other humans in my realm don't have that. I can help change their minds, so they don't come. At least, I promise to try."

Indigo hadn't thought of that case, but she was right. Other humans might cross over, and it would be awful. But as a burrow mate she would be more effective in stopping them.

"She must be banished," the predator tortoise thought.

Indigo sent her a sharp thought. "You won't do well either, if other sapient humans come. None of us will. You're better off letting us keep our burrow, where we can block off the portal. We couldn't do it without Rowan—and neither could you. You could be destroyed, if you are there when they come. They have frightening—" His thought stalled, because he lacked enough of the concept.

"Machines," Rowan thought helpfully. "Including weapons that can kill any animals from a distance."

"Weapons?" the coyote asked.

"Guns," Rowan thought with distaste. She made a mental picture of a coyote and a man. Something flashed in the man's hand, and the coyote fell dead. "They hurl bits of metal that hurt what they hit." She amplified the concept of guns and bullets. They were terrible things.

That set the predator tortoise back. She consulted with her burrow mates. All of them were shaken by Rowan's revelation, which they knew was a true one. Then she addressed the Elder. "We withdraw our protest."

The Elders consulted, and came to their decision. "The sapient human is approved as a burrow mate. Your burrow is recognized. But we may reconsider later, if your sapient human does not keep others out."

And there it was: victory. Indigo reveled in the joy of Rowan's mind, that they all shared.

But the Elder was not quite finished. He addressed Gopher. "And we will be looking for evidence that you have become a responsible landlord and burrow leader. Your

wild days must end. Burrow management is serious business."

Now Rowan laughed. "Tortoise reform! You can't avoid
it any more."

Indigo knew that was going to be difficult for Gopher.
And for the rest of them. They were all young and wild.

Author's Note

This novel is fiction, of course, but it is drawn from reality. I live on a small tree farm in Florida, and all the animals of the home burrow are there. Gopher tortoises really do dig burrows, anywhere up to forty feet long, and perhaps ten feet deep. They spend most of their time in them, coming out mainly to graze on wire grass and some leafed plants. There are tortoise burrows all along our long drive, and two are right by our house, so we see the tortoises often enough. Each one has a slightly different pattern on its shell, so they can be told apart. We like them, and leave them alone, because that's the way they prefer it.

Other animals do join the tortoises in their burrows. The small burrowing owl does, and the indigo snake, and over a hundred other creatures. So the gopher tortoise really is a landlord, and without his burrow a number of other animals would be in trouble. The gopher tortoise is thus a keystone species—that is, one whose presence fundamentally affects the welfare of other animals. That is one reason it is a protected species. Once upon a time people hunted these tortoises and ate them; now that is forbidden.

What does not exist, as far as we know, is telepathy. So I wrote this story to explore what it might be like if there were a realm where animals could read each other's minds, not needing to talk the way human beings do. If they could do that, they would have a great advantage, and might even be able to form an animal civilization. If they learned to read minds long enough ago—millions of years—they might have taken over the world, and human beings would never have had the chance. Perhaps that would be a better world.

—*Piers Anthony, October, 2004*

Piers Anthony is one of the world's most prolific and popular authors. His fantasy Xanth novels have been read and loved by millions of readers around the world, and have appeared on the *New York Times* Best Seller list 21 times.

Although Piers is mostly known for fantasy and science fiction, he has written novels in other genres as well, including historical fiction, martial arts, and horror.

Piers Anthony's official website is HI PIERS at www.hipiers.com, where he publishes his bi-monthly online newsletter. Piers lives with his wife in Central Florida.

Printed in the United Kingdom
by Lightning Source UK Ltd.
127791UK00001B/74/A